CALL IN THE FEDS!

Borgo Press Books by GORDON LANDSBOROUGH

Call in the Feds!: A Classic Suspense Novel
F.B.I. Showdown: A Classic Suspense Novel

CALL IN THE FEDS!

A CLASSIC SUSPENSE NOVEL

GORDON LANDSBOROUGH

THE BORGO PRESS

MMXII

CALL IN THE FEDS!

FIRST BORGO PRESS EDITION

Published by Wildside Press LLC

www.wildsidebooks.com

DEDICATION

For my daughter, Bonny

CONTENTS

CHAPTER ONE: PRETTY BOY ARRIVES 9

CHAPTER TWO: TIME-LOCK. 17

CHAPTER THREE: CALL IN THE FEDS!. . . . 27

CHAPTER FOUR: PARTNER IN CRIME 39

CHAPTER FIVE: BOSS MYRTLE

    INTERVENES 51

CHAPTER SIX: PRETTY BOY 67

CHAPTER SEVEN: G-MEN 73

CHAPTER EIGHT: THE NET CLOSES 85

CHAPTER NINE: WHERE'S BONNIE? 93

CHAPTER TEN: VIGILANTES RETURN . . . 105

CHAPTER ELEVEN: PRETTY BOY GETS

    AN IDEA 119

CHAPTER TWELVE: ROADBLOCK

    CARNAGE 131

CHAPTER THIRTEEN: SATIATION. 143

CHAPTER FOURTEEN: WHEN THE SAFE
    OPENED 153
ABOUT THE AUTHOR 163

CHAPTER ONE
PRETTY BOY ARRIVES

Abruptly, the phone bell broke into harsh discordance, shattering the quiet of the smoke-filled, sunlit office high up in the police building.

The big young police captain dropped his feet quickly from his desk, startled. He said, "My God, if you don't get that cracked bell seen to, it'll give me the jeebies one day!"

The two police clerks went on writing. They heard his voice. He said: "Yeah?" Then another casual, "Yeah." And then they heard him jump to his feet, his voice rising abruptly when he spoke: "Sure, sure. I'll be right down. Get a car."

They turned. Captain Harlan Just slammed the phone back on the desk, then grabbed for hat and gun.

One cynical deskman said to the other, "It's a horse-fly bit him." The other said, "He ain't no horse." And he made it sound as though he wasn't certain.

At the door Lanny Just turned and startled them into silence. He rapped: "He's been seen, down at the rail station."

The cops started to get their fat lips around a big

"Who?" but the head of the Freshwater Detective Division spoke again, first. "Him," he almost shouted. And then, to make sure: *"Him!"*

And then they knew and were suitably shocked.

The police car started moving as he raced across the sidewalk. The door swung open and he went in, head down like a quarterback. The swift, fierce acceleration threw him against the other occupant of the rear seat, and it took him seconds to fight for his balance against the increasing momentum. Then he got into a seat, shoved his hat back, saw a red face and black eyebrows, and the day went sour for him.

"Why the hell?" he began, and then shut his mouth.

They had a hundred and sixteen cops in Freshwater, ten of them sergeants—and they had to pick on Sergeant Aubie Gillis to accompany him on this trip!

Gillis! Lanny could have spat at the thought. Gillis, a crooked cop if ever there was one.

Gillis was watching him, just the suggestion of a grin on that hard face that was as red-raw as the beef on the hooks in the down-town abattoir. A cunning, watchful face, but bold and brutal.

Lanny snarled, "Hell, you...." Then viciously, "Well, there'll be no pickings for you on this case."

The hard-faced cop's eyes slanted. "Meanin'?"

"Meanin' nothin'." Lanny gave back look for look, After a few seconds, the sergeant turned his head and squinted along the tree-lined boulevard that led to the terminus of the New York-Freshwater Railroad.

Lanny heard Gillis' voice come trickling out of the

side of his mouth. "You're out to nail me. Well, watch your step. You got nothin' on me...."

The police captain let the sneer flow like syrup round his words as the car screamed on protesting tyres up the station approach. "Me, I'm out to nail nobody—only crooked cops. If you were straight, Gillis, you'd have nothing to fear; but you're one of those grafting cops the people of Freshwater are gunning for, and you'll get no mercy from me."

They were stopping. Lanny just tumbled out of the car, leaving his assistant dumb. Just now there was something more important to do than bicker with a two-timing police-sergeant. *He* was reported to have been seen in Freshwater.

Another train had just pulled in from the city, and the big police-captain had to force his way against a river of newly-arrived vacationers. They ran to bright clothes, brighter ties, loud voices, and louder children, and the noise was bewildering under the glass-roofed station front.

Lanny got through at last, Sergeant Gillis and a patrolman hard behind. And back in the station yard two more patrol cars came tearing in, sirens screaming a peremptory demand for right of way.

A uniformed man saw Lanny and came quickly across. He was the man who had phoned in the report—one of the railroad's private police. He was an old-timer, an ex-regular, and pretty reliable, Lanny knew.

He grabbed him and shoved him out of the way of the tail end of the departing stream of vacationers.

"Let's have it," he rapped.

Joe MacReady had a paper in his hand, was already unfolding it. "I don't make mistakes," he bragged. "I saw him here 'bout ten minutes ago."

He was stabbing a picture on the front sheet of the newspaper, his finger punctuating his every word. "He was up there at the cigar stand, talking to the girl. I wasn't sure at first, so I tried to work round him."

"And he got away in the crowd?"

The railroad cop nodded. He was looking hard at the picture. "But not before I was sure. That's him. It's him, I tell you—he's tryin' to hole out here in Freshwater."

Other cops had come up now, and people were stopping to stare at the group of police in the big hallway. They knew something was in the wind, and a ripple of excitement ran along the crowd as they watched the quickly conferring group.

MacReady said, "As soon as I lost him, I got through to you." Lanny nodded approval. He was planning the next move. He thought: That girl at the tobacco kiosk. I must speak to her. He remembered her. A nice kid if movie-mad.

He said, "We're wasting time here. Jeter, you get through to the chief. Tell him I'm satisfied that Pretty Boy's been seen here in Freshwater." MacReady preened. Lanny whirled on him. "Mac, I haven't many men, so you've got to stay on your feet here at the station until Pretty Boy's behind bars. You know him; you've got to check on every outgoing passenger from this station to make sure he doesn't get away. Got that? Pretty Boy's turned up in Freshwater, and by God we're goin' to keep him here."

He started moving back to the station exit. The crowd parted this time to let them through. Someone said softly, as they passed, "What's cookin', bud?" And a big mouth yapped, "Pretty Boy," before Lanny could stop him.

The captain snarled at the patrolman, "You dumb cluck! How long now d'you think it'll be before Pretty Boy wises to the fact that we know he's here in Freshwater? What the hell, you tryin' to help him?"

He told one car to get down to the pier. "There's the afternoon coast steamer going out in a coupla hours. Don't let it sail until you're sure our man's not aboard," was his instruction, then he climbed into his own car.

"What now?" asked Sergeant Gillis. He had forgotten the feud that had recently developed between him and his Superior. Anyway, there was no graft in Pretty Boy, not for Gillis.

"Back to headquarters." Lanny was thinking: All that way just to watch a fellow's face while he tells you what he's already said over the phone. But that's how you had to do it in police work. Anyone could ring up, and a phone call didn't sound convincing. But sight of MacReady's face while he was repeating his story had been sufficient.

Pretty Boy, New York's latest sensational criminal, was in Freshwater City, this playground on the Atlantic coast. Lanny, anyway, had few doubts about it now, and you didn't bother about doubts when there was a chance of hooking on to Pretty Boy....

A patrolman had picked up a new edition outside the station. Lanny reached forward and grabbed it. But now he was giving orders to Patrolman Jeter at the radio.

"Tell the chief I want every man recalled to duty. Tell him every man stays on his feet until we know we've got Pretty Boy—or lost him. Tell him I want a cordon thrown right round the city—every road out must have a block. Call out the Vigilantes to help— they can watch across the fields and back roads. Keep a watch out at the airport. Tell him the station's covered and a car's down at the pier head. Tell him if Pretty Boy's in Freshwater, he won't get out!"

Jeter's voice jumped into harsh, staccato repetition, and the orders were radioed through to the chief. As they came into the back road leading to the police HQ, a flurry of motorcycle cops came leaning crazily round the corners, heads down, tyres biting a precarious hold at that speed, sirens shrieking. Lanny saw them tear north along the Boston highway, and then they were in the yard and he was out and up the stairs three at a time.

The chief was on his feet as he crashed into the room. He was shouting, "Here's something else for you, Lanny. It's your busy day."

Lanny grabbed the message form and skimmed it through. Then he said, "Jesus sneezes!" and the newspaper dropped forgotten from his hand as he raced back down the stairs.

The chief gazed down. A handsome face looked up at him from the newspaper. Pretty Boy's. And bold type shouted out a headline consisting of two words—

MANIAC MURDERER

CHAPTER TWO
TIME-LOCK

He was Alan Ladd again. He stood in the warm sunshine, with his back against the wall of the bank. The brim of his hat was low across his eyes, and his hands were thrust deep inside his belted gabardine.

Inside the car Gino Lucci, stick-up man, said, "Fer Crissakes, he don't have to look like he's gonna rob a bank, does he?"

Eddy Eitel growled, "The dope.... It's them movies he lives in." He moved impatiently. These last three minutes were going slower'n hell, though the other two didn't seem to be affected by the waiting.

There was Bright, back of the car. He had another name, but Bright suited him because he wasn't more than half-bright. He was a cretin, with high cheekbones and hair-tufted warts and eyes that looked uncertainly two ways at once. Just now, as always, his thin-lipped gash of a mouth was twitching back from broken teeth, baring them into a crazy, half-witted grin.

But Bright could use a gun if only someone was at hand to tell him when to shoot. And that kind of loon is useful in a stick-up gang.

The driver, Maxie Christman, just sat behind the wheel, a huddled, silent, brooding question mark, his eyes apathetically looking along the main shopping street of this suburb of Freshwater.

The tall, lean man in the gabardine moved slightly now. His eyes almost hidden between narrowed lids, he was looking into the bank. He could see the bank janitor, close by the door—a clock that gave less than a minute to closing time. And the clerks and customers beyond.

And today there weren't many customers. There never were on Fridays, for some reason, a fact which Gino had soon noticed when he'd started to watch this bank. No more than six or eight in there right now, and that wasn't too many to handle.

The spotter stiffened as the janitor looked up at the bank clock and then started to cross to the door. He had a big bunch of keys in his hands. At once the man in the gabardine turned and walked into the bank.

Gino got out of the car and crossed the sidewalk. He got in the way of the janitor and held him up for a second, and that gave Eddy Eitel and the cretin Bright time to get out and follow him.

The janitor was surprised at the last-minute flood of customers—and they were strangers. He looked at the clock again and opened his mouth to say something about the time, but Bright, his face grinning like a dog's drooling with distemper, slammed something hard into his ribs and that shut him up.

Eddy grabbed the keys, quickly pushed the door

to and locked it. A heavy, middle-aged man with an unhealthy face saw it happen. He had a handful of greenbacks of small denomination. He called, uncertainly, "Hey, what's the idea?" scenting something was wrong.

Four guns came out at that.

Gino and the man in the gabardine were already at the grill. Gino shoved his gun through and snapped, "That alarm button on the floor. I know it's there. But just try usin' it. Go on, try it!"

But none of the bank employees did. They looked at the guns, they looked at each other, then they silently put their hands above their heads. Gino said, "You guys got brains. Cover 'em an' if they move, blow them brains out for 'em, Alan Ladd!"

The man in the gabardine crouched behind his gun, a figure tense and menacing. The clerks stood, taut and staring. They knew that here was a man who would use his gun...might even be wanting an opportunity to use it. And they didn't intend to give him an excuse.

The handful of bank customers stood rigid close against the heavy, polished counter. They were all middle-aged, unprepossessing, tradesman types. And by the way they looked, they all knew what a gun could do.

Bright was covering them from by the door, Eddy Eitel having gone forward; and Bright was disconcerting, because his eyes seemed able to watch up and down the room simultaneously.

Gino went round the counter. He didn't hurry. There

was no need to. He had watched this bank so long he was pretty sure he'd got it thoroughly cased by now. It was bank closing time, and with that door locked behind them they were safe from unexpected interruption.

He pulled off the wires leading to the two alarm devices, then prodded his gun into the side of one of the clerks. The man gasped as it took the wind out of him. Gino liked the sound and prodded again.

"Over to that safe," he ordered. "You others follow." When they were inside the safe—so big, in reality it was a strong room—he said, "We want all the bills up to a hundred dollars. The rest you can have for yourselves. Now, stick 'em into this sack here."

Eddy Eitel went swiftly over the customers and removed the cash they had just drawn from the bank. It didn't amount to much, and he muttered "Pikers," contemptuously, and then started to shove them round the counter. The unhealthy-looking bank client looked bad and was breathing labouredly through lips that were going blue.

Gino looked round when he found the mob of middle-aged tradesmen treading on his heels. He wagged his gun and growled, "Hold it, punks. I ain't ready for you—yet." The tradesmen didn't like the way he came out with the last word.

For that matter they didn't like Gino. He looked what he was—scum. Something out of Italy, formless with soft fat—greasy-skinned, large-pored, a fat, flat, sallow face with a smear of moustache across it. He was a dandy with his rings and the silk scarf tucked into his shirt collar, though he hadn't got round to shaving that day. That was like Gino—lazy. That was why he had taken to crime—working seemed tedious to the Italian immigrant.

He and Eddy Eitel were running this gang between them, though neither had brains amounting to anything. They were just a pair of crude guns able to organise a stick-up....

Bright came shoving his drooling, grinning, half-witted face round the corner. "I ain't killed nobody so far. Ain't nobody gonna be killed on this job?" he mouthed. Bright had killed a few men in his time, so he'd told them. He had been vague about the details, so they weren't sure. Gino had picked him up recently because they'd lost a fellow when a mechanic in a filling station they were sticking up unexpectedly came at them with a gun. For a bank robbery it was safer to have four guns and a driver.

Some of the tradesmen thought he was kidding, because it seemed too crude, that speech about killing someone. Then the loon fanned them with bad breath from between grinning, broken teeth and they saw the wildness in his wandering eyes and they weren't so sure.

Gino just grunted and said, "I got it all." He took hold of the sack that had been stuffed with notes.

Eddy said, quickly, "How much d'you reckon?"

Gino shrugged. "Maybe twenty gee. Maybe more." Then he wagged his gun at the crowding, silent bank customers. "Inside, you!" he ordered.

They looked surprised. The bank clerks had started to come out of the big safe, but Gino's gun stopped them. The four gangsters backed away and covered the little group with their guns.

"Get inside," Gino ordered, "else I'll sic my dawg on you." He indicated Bright, open-mouthed and expectant behind his gun. Bright with his finger straining eagerly at the trigger. And they understood and shuffled back hurriedly. The blue-lipped man was having to be held up; he was in pretty bad shape. Eddy saw the janitor and one of the bank employees in front of the big safe and said, "you, too," and they stepped back quickly.

Bright shambled forward a pace, disappointed. "Don't we kill just one?" he pleaded. There was no doubt he meant it. It made Eddy Eidel look quickly across at Gino, but he didn't seem to be bothered by it.

The squat, shapeless Italian stepped forward when they were all inside the strong room. He put his shoulder to the massive door and started to close it. The men inside in the strong room panicked at that.

"You can't do that," shouted one of the bank employees, probably the manager. "My God, you don't know what you're doing. There's a time-lock on that door. If it's closed, we can't get out till eight tomorrow morning."

Gino said, casually, "That, brother, is the idea," and moved the door faster.

There was frenzied commotion at that. Suddenly every man inside the strong room found his voice.

Above the commotion they heard the janitor's voice suddenly appealing.

"There's a mighty sick man here. You gotta do something for him...."

Bright slavered eagerly, "Let's kill'm. Jes' one shot, huh?"

But Gino rushed the door to. There was a metallic, clicking sound, and immediately the bank was quiet. The door must have been soundproofed.

Gino looked round. He scooped the small change out from the tills, put it in his pocket and then changed his mind and took most of it out again. It was chicken-feed and weighed too heavily in his coat.

Then they walked across to the street door and Eddy briskly opened it. They came out into the sunshine in a group, Gino calling over his shoulder, "Sure, sure. And thanks a lot, bud. We won't make it so late next time."

That was for the benefit of the few passers-by. It looked good, natural, and no one gave more than a glance at the stick-up men. The door shut and locked automatically behind them.

They got into their car and Maxie drove steadily away. There was no hurry. Properly handled, a daylight bank robbery is a comparatively simple affair, and this was probably a better hold-up than most. Probably it would be several hours before the alarm was raised— it might not he until the following morning, in fact— and long before dark they expected to be within the friendly jungle of New York's East Side.

So they tooled steadily along the seaside resort's

tree-lined boulevard, obeying every traffic law like good citizens; and they felt at peace with the world because they had a sack full of notes that were probably untraceable because of their small value.

Gino preened and felt himself a big-shot mobster. This was better than sticking up filling stations, with crazy mechanics running loose with guns.

Only Bright was disconsolate. He said, vaguely, "We didn't kill no one. You said to be ready to kill, Gino, but no one did nothin' wrong. Ain't we gonna have some excitement?"

Eddy shot out of the corner of his mouth, "By cripes, Gino, the buzzard means it. Where in hell did you dig him up? He's dangerous, that guy."

Gino was picking his teeth—the car was tooling along as smoothly as all that. They were coming out of the town now, and feeling better with every minute of that lovely afternoon that passed. He sucked a tooth clean and then said back, "Aw, Bright's all right. He ain't quite bright, maybe, but what the hell do you want on a job like this? Einstein?"

Eddy muttered, "You can't tell, with these birdbrains. You never know what they'll do—"

Maxie Christman ceased to he a living question mark over the driving wheel. His body straightened as he stood on the brake pedal, became instead an exclamation mark.

They found themselves crashing forward as the car's momentum was suddenly zeroed, heard Maxie's voice bellow back at them, "A trap!"

Just round the bend where the road joined the river valley a car was pulled across the highway. Men were climbing out. They wore uniforms.

"Cops!" snarled Eddy, but there was bewilderment in his tone. How could the cops have got to know of the bank hold-up so quickly? Then he leaned forward. Speculation could be left till later; just now they were in a jam and had to get themselves out of it.

Eddy could act quickly. Now he grabbed Maxie's shoulder and rapped, "Ram that car, then turn and go back!"

That was the programme. No good trying to turn here, within eighty yards of the cops. Those cops carried guns, and anyway, long before they'd got their car pointing back into Freshwater the cop car would have swung round and caught up with them.

Put the cop car out of action—and hope to God it didn't put their car out, too! That was the programme.

Maxie opened up instantly and the heavy gang car leapt into violent acceleration. They saw the cops scatter, and it was obvious that the move was unexpected and they were thrown off their stride.

Then the mobster's car crashed head on into the side of the sleek, speedy police car. Glass splintered, metal tore. Above the noise Eddy shouted, "Back, Maxie. Reverse...."

The car tore itself away from the shattered cop car, and went plunging recklessly in reverse. The police lugged out guns and started to fire. Eddy heard a crack close to his ear and saw a cop grab his stomach and go down.

"What the—?" he swore and turned and looked into Bright's tight-grinning face. Heard Bright saying, "Gee, I did for him. Right in the belly. Gee, bet he don't feel so good with that in him." His eyes were going all over the place in excitement.

Eddy snarled, "Goddam you, you don't kill cops like people. Cops is different. It'll make 'em mad, and we ain't in no position to make cops mad."

Not at this moment, turning the car in the only direction they could go, back into Freshwater. Freshwater—a town at the end of a line, as New Yorkers called them.

A trap, if all roads out were watched, and they guessed they would be.

CHAPTER THREE
CALL IN THE FEDS!

As they sirened their way out of town. Lanny saw an ambulance pull on to the road just ahead. It beat them to the river road by a hundred yards.

There was a traffic jam just round the bend, with cars being examined by harassed cops and then going awkwardly over rough ground to get around the shattered police car. There was someone wrapped in some coats on the ground by the rear wheel of the wrecked car, and as Lanny got out he saw stretcher-bearers and white-coated interns run across to the fallen patrolman.

Lanny put his men on to clearing the road, to help the two squad men, and went across to speak to the sergeant of the squad car. It was Alec Pedersen, a blond athlete and a pretty square guy in a town of crooked cops.

Lanny said, "Well, sergeant, how is he?"

Pedersen didn't look happy. He said, "There was a doctor in one of those cars. He says he hasn't a hope in hell. Don't reckon he'll survive the ride back to hospital."

They watched while the stretcher was skilfully slid

under the injured patrolman; then he was lifted and carried gently across to the ambulance. They were having to hurry. There wasn't much life left.

They got him in and started to shut the doors. The ambulance didn't move.

Lanny said, "It was Kippax, Ronnie Kippax, wasn't it?"

Pedersen nodded. "He was quite a good guy," he epitaphed. Lanny didn't say anything because he wasn't so sure. Most of these cops were grafters, he had found; perhaps even Pedersen, on the quiet.

One of the interns came down the ambulance steps. He slipped off his rubber gloves slowly. He wasn't hurrying at all now. Lanny strode across to him.

The intern said, casually, "You got a murder case on your hands, captain."

"He died?"

"Just now."

Lanny wheeled on Pedersen. "Your radio's still okay?" Pedersen nodded. "Then get through to HQ. Tell them that Patrolman Kippax just died. They'll know what to do." Pedersen lingered. "The F.B.I.?"

"Sure. It's a Federal offence to kill a cop in the United States. It's now a job for G-men. We can get back to our job of tracking Pretty Boy."

When Pedersen came back from radioing HQ, Lanny said. "Now, tell me what happened."

Pedersen took off his hat and wiped the band. Lanny noticed how thin the sergeant was getting on top, though he was still in his early twenties. He said,

"We got a radio call from HQ saying Pretty Boy was in town and for us to block the New York road. We were outside Marty's Tavern, so it only took us half a minute to get here and pull across the road.

"Well, first car that comes along is some old boy who might have been pretty a long time back. Next, a black Pontiac came tooling round the bend. We weren't ready for what happened. Suddenly it accelerated and drove straight into our car, then went back in reverse. We tried to stop it with a bullet in the tyres, but I guess we weren't aiming too steady and it just went on. Then someone fired a gun from the back of the car and Kippax went down, screaming his guts out. The car turned, out of range, and went on back into Freshwater."

He looked at the wrecked car. "We couldn't do a thing. That wing's crushed against the tyre and so we couldn't use the car. And it was a couple of minutes before anyone else drove up. So I got through to HQ and reported the matter."

"That's one good thing," said Lanny. "It didn't wreck the radio. They're pretty well trapped, now."

The police maintenance wagon came screaming up just then, and Lanny went back to his car. Pedersen followed. He seemed to want to talk.

He said, "They won't get away?"

Lanny shrugged. "I don't see how. Thanks to Pretty Boy, every road out of town is watched, and so's the pier, railroad, and airport. And Freshwater's not such a big place."

Pedersen stood with one foot on the front tyre. He was still wanting to talk. Lanny didn't get in yet.

"Any idea who they might be?"

Lanny exploded, "Jesus Christ, what a question! They operate like New York gunnies, but we don't have them around Freshwater that I know of." Except Myrtle's mob, he could have added, but didn't.

"Maybe they've pulled some job in town and were on their way out?"

"Maybe. But we haven't had word of any big job being pulled in the last hour or so," returned Lanny. Then he said, exasperated again, "This is a day! Pretty Boy is seen in town, and within minutes someone goes and shoots a cop—a gang of gunnies!"

"You don't think they're connected?"

"I don't. Pretty Boy's no professional criminal. He's got the killer lust, and he doesn't kill prettily, at that. But you don't get that kind running around with a bunch of hoods. No, this is coincidence, sergeant."

And then he said, abruptly, "Now tell me what's on your mind, Pedersen."

Pedersen took his foot off the tyre, startled by the directness of the order. He was flustered, spoke defensively. "I don't get you, captain—"

Lanny shoved his face close up to the sergeant's. He was bigger than Pedersen, broader, dark-haired where the sergeant was blond; more aggressive in his manner...a more intelligent, more dangerous man.

He said, "You've been trying to say something for the last five minutes, Pedersen. Why don't you come

out with it? Think you might he talking out of turn?"
There was a rasp of unpleasantness in his voice.

Pedersen suddenly looked him squarely in the eyes.
"That's it, captain. I'm goin' to talk out of turn. Look,
when I first started on patrol I used to get things given
me. You know, parcels of fruit and meat and groceries,
and lifts out to the races. We all get them, don't we?"

Lanny nodded, his face hard. Pedersen squinted
after the departing ambulance and said, "Of course the
idea's to soften us up in case there's something a little
bit wrong at times—if they park their cars where they
shouldn't, you know."

Lanny got impatient. "Sure, sure, I know all that.
And I know that after a time the presents get a bit
bigger and you've to earn them. Like money from a
bookie, or a softener from a ladies' house, huh?"

Pedersen kept his eyes down the road. He said,
"Sure, you know how it is. You don't know how far
you've gone until it's got a bit late to do anything."

Lanny said, "Now tell me what all this adds up to?"
And then he knew he was speaking to an honest cop,
even though he had taken softeners.

For Pedersen said, impatiently, "I know what I've
done, and I'm prepared to take what comes for it. Not
that I've got in deep. But I keep thinking, and I don't
reckon to a lot of no-goods and politicians running a
police force. I'd like to see the place cleaned up. And I
reckon you're the man that can do it, and wants to do it
after that Alastair Myrtle business."

He looked round. No one was near. "I'll give you

a tip, captain. Watch your step. They know you're dangerous, because you can't be bought. But these grafters are making too much dough out of Freshwater, and they won't let a police captain stand in the way. You'll have to go, captain, and the grape vine says they've started moving in on you already."

Lanny kept watching that fresh, pink face, and Pedersen all the time kept his eyes up the road.

He asked, "How do you know all this? And what do they intend to do?"

Pedersen shrugged. "There are whispers, that's all. Nothing you can pin anyone down to, but they add up, all the same. Just things some of our no-good cops let fall when someone mentions your name. I guess a whole parcel of Freshwater cops is in Boss Myrtle's pocket."

"Yeah," Lanny growled. "And don't I know it."

He was thinking of Alastair Myrtle, Boss Myrtle's brother. Thinking of what happened less than a week ago.

He'd been cruising in a squad car with Sergeant Aubie Gillis and a couple of patrolmen down town. They'd seen a couple of big cars parked down the Waterway, and Lanny recognized the licence plate of one of them. Boss Myrtle's own car.

The cars were so big, there was no room to pass, and Lanny had got out to find the drivers. They were in back of Jules Stedmann's ramshackle old shop—Stedmann the gunsmith who had offered to supply arms to the newly-formed Freshwater Vigilance Committee. And they were beating the daylights out of him.

Jules wasn't pretty, with his face bruised and puffy and leaking blood out of his nose and corners of his mouth. A couple of Boss Myrtle's over-fed apes were holding him, while Alastair Myrtle worked on him with a piece of rubber.

He was beating old Jules across the face, and he wore his usual expression of grim good humour. He was a fine-built man, erect and military, with a big, handsome brown face, and a neatly waxed moustache; his clothes were sporty and the best that a New York tailor could supply.

Lanny came out with his gun, and Aubie Gillis and a patrolman who had followed in case someone had to be booked, came out with theirs, too.

Alastair Myrtle looked across with amusement and casually gave old Jules another blow across the ear. Jules sagged as if that last blow had been too much for his powers of resistance.

Lanny rapped, "Do that again. Myrtle, and you won't use your arm for a month."

Myrtle for answer threw the hose on to the floor and said, "And you're not kidding! Okay, I won't take you up on it. We'll go now, boys. C'mon."

He found Lanny behind a gun blocking his way. Jules found strength in his legs again and stood up. He looked a wreck. Alastair looked down at the gun as though there was a joke attached to it. He said, "Now, captain, that doesn't look friendly."

Lanny's voice clipped, "Who says I feel friendly,

seeing you beating up an old guy like that? I'm gonna book you, so get moving out to the car."

Two more apes came in from the workroom that overhung the creek. One was carrying a shotgun with a splintered stock. Lanny thought: So that's it. They're wrecking the place. They don't want an armed Vigilance Committee here in Freshwater.

But Alastair Myrtle didn't turn a hair. He said, "My lawyer will want to know the charge, so let's be knowing it now."

Lanny's eyes glinted. He'd had truck with Boss Myrtle's brother before. "I'm booking you on a charge of assault."

Alastair Myrtle turned with infinite leisure, surveyed old Jules and then looked at his companions. He said, with an air of surprise, "Now, that beats everything. Nobody's been assaulted here, has there?"

His apes relaxed into confident grins and shuffled with awkward good-humour while they shook their heads. Jules didn't say anything. Alastair Myrtle spoke to him directly.

"You don't say anything, Stedmann. But you don't remember seeing anyone assaulted, do you? Better think carefully before you answer." The voice was pleasant, but there was a leavening of significance in the tone, and Jules got it first time.

He lifted his head tiredly. "No," he said. "Nobody ain't bin beat up that I remember. Ain't bin no assault, captain...."

He said it even though he could hardly get the words

through his bruised mouth, and then he sagged again and passed out.

Lanny said. "Intimidation of a witness, huh? Well, you're still going through on a charge of assault, Myrtle. Three witnesses saw you beating up this old man—me and my men. We don't need Stedmann's corroboration. Now, get moving!"

Alastair Myrtle shrugged resignedly, and without any apparent loss of equanimity he went out to the police car.

An hour later Lanny was summoned to the police chief's office. The chief, an old man brought up in the school of crooked Tammany politics, announced abruptly, "You'd better withdraw your charge against Alastair Myrtle, captain."

"Why?" Lanny's narrowed eyes were hostile.

The chief leaned forward heavily. "Because you might as well. You'll never make it stick. There's only your word against half a dozen witnesses who're saying you've been imagining things."

"Myrtle and his apes?" Then softly, because he knew the answer—"But what about Sergeant Gillis and the patrolmen? They saw as much as I did."

The chief looked at a lot of things around the room and then suddenly his eyes came back and met his subordinate's. Harshly he said, "They tell me they never saw a thing. Stedmann says he fell down the stairs and some customers were giving him treatment when you came in. Gillis says all they saw was Stedmann being supported by Myrtle's men. So your charge wouldn't stick, captain."

"I get it." Lanny rose slowly. He looked very big silhouetted against the wide window that overlooked the bay. He said, "Myrtle—or his brother—have got at my men."

The chief said, unpleasantly, "Better be careful what you say, captain."

Lanny put his hands on the desk, and leaned forward so that his hard grey eyes were within inches of his chief's. His voice had the bite of a hand saw. "Chief, you know it as well as I do. They've been got at. And it isn't the first time Boss Myrtle's racketeers have twisted the law as they wanted it. This town's sick of graft and corruption and they won't stand for much more. They think so little of Freshwater police that they've revived the old Vigilance Committee—and those old-timers mean business. Well, I'm with them, and by God, if it's the last thing I do, I'm going to run the whole stinking mob in!"

He strode across to the door, then paused. When he turned his face was hard. "Maybe you'll pass that message on to Boss Myrtle," he said bitingly.

It stung. The chief came leaping out of his chair, glaring.

"By God, captain, I won't stand for that sort of talk. Are you saying I'm in Myrtle's pocket?"

It was bluster, and both knew it. Lanny just growled a contemptuous, "You should know," and went out.

And now Sergeant Pedersen was telling him that the Myrtle Machine was after him—out to remove him because of that threat he had made to his chief.

He got into his car. Pedersen lingered even then. And then, just as he was about to be driven away, Pedersen stooped and said, softly, "Captain, if there's a jam, count on me. I'm sick to hell of this graft. And there's a few boys I know you can depend on."

Lanny's hard face relaxed into a grim smile. "Thanks, sergeant. That's something to remember, I guess."

The radio was talking. They listened. "Captain Just to report immediately back to HQ. Captain Just to withdraw the Vigilance pickets right away." The message was repeated.

Pedersen gave a tight grin and said, "This is it, captain. Betcha that's the squeeze starting right away."

He saluted and walked quickly away. Lanny nodded for the car to start. The radio was talking again.

A Pontiac with shattered windows and a crumpled front had been found down by the pier head. A patrolman had found witnesses who had seen five men get out and walk quickly away. They gave pretty good descriptions, and these came over the air in a general broadcast to all cars.

They were driving back to town as the news came over the air. Lanny at once started giving orders.

All roadblocks should move in on the town, tightening the net. Vigilantes would also move up with the police, he ordered.

His men looked quickly at him when he gave this latter order, but it went out all the same. The driver said, "HQ?"

Lanny said. "No, we're going into the old town, round the seafront. We're gonna comb through the dives and doss-houses and see if we can drive these gunnies into the open." Then he grinned. "I never heard that order, and maybe you'd like to forget you heard it, too."

The men just looked ahead and said nothing. Lanny thought: It's hell, not being able to trust your own men.

CHAPTER FOUR
PARTNER IN CRIME

Gino Lucci was worried and his brown Italian eyes showed it. He watched the concrete highway speed towards the Pontiac's wheels and he said, "We gotta ditch this can quick. That bust nose won't get us nowhere but trouble."

Eddy Eitel stopped snarling to say. "The hell, who brought this trouble on us. anyway? Fer Crissakes, what for you brought that screwball into the party, you—"

Gino took it for a few seconds and then got worked up on his own account. "You said for to get a guy who wouldn't mind using a rod, didn't you? So what? So I got one. That lame brain's kinda impulsive and we oughta took his gun from him when we came outa the bank."

"Sure, sure," jeered Eddy. "Sure we oughta done a lotta things. *Like keepin' the buzzard outa this party!*"

Bright heard but just grinned amiably. Next to him Boy Fehse, looking more like Alan Ladd than ever, sat hunched in the corner, his hand holding something under his armpit. Eddy's lip curled as he saw him. Bright and Boy Fehse weren't real hoods like him and

Gino ant Maxie Christman. In their way, both were screwballs....

Suddenly he leaned forward and rapped, "Pull off the highway at the crossing. There's a road leads down to the harbour, missing the town. We'll ditch the car down there."

"And then?" Maxie didn't know Freshwater like Gino and Eddy had come to know it in the past week.

Eddy thought rapidly. "We gotta get away from this can first. Then we gotta hide up until we know how to get outa this burg. By now they'll sure have every road watched outa town." He looked viciously at the drooling Bright on the back seat.

"So?"

"So I know a place where we can stay. When we get out string along behind me. Don't look as if we're together, see?"

They nodded. They were descending a narrow winding street that grew meaner and more sordid the nearer they came to the sea front. The neighbourhood looked tough, and the sidewalks were thronged with seamen of many nations. It had a homely look about it, and for the first time since the shooting the mobsters felt cheered.

Suddenly Maxie stood on his brakes. Right ahead were the white-painted timber railings that guarded the pier head. Maxie rapped, "Cops. See dat cop can— Jeez, they bin quick!"

Eddy was already getting out. The others followed. Eddy turned and went back a few yards, then crossed the street and entered a side turning. The others came at irregular intervals behind him. Boy Fehse was walking with his hand under his armpit, until Maxie Christman came up and cursed him for the goddam show-off he was, and at that he snarled but took his hand out and instead shoved it deep into his gabardine pocket. Gino caught up with Maxie who complained, "What the hell, why did we have to pick on that pair of crap wits?"

Gino said nothing. It seemed that Maxie and Eddy were both trying to put the finger on him for the miscarriage of their plot.

Eddy turned out into the bigger, busier street beyond, in such a hurry that he bumped into a fellow who was coming across the sidewalk into a store. The fellow said something in a Limey accent, but Eddy didn't catch it and went on.

A few yards up the street he looked round quickly and then went up some worn, metal-treaded stairs. He waited at the top until the others joined him, and then went down a dull, dirty passage until they came to the end door. An apathetic card loosely tacked up announced that this was the registered office of Freshwater Shippers, Inc.

Eddy turned the handle and walked straight in. The others crowded quickly in after him. A girl looked up from a typewriter and said, "Some guys knock when they come into an office." She was startled by the suddenness of their arrival, was hostile because of it.

Eddy said, smoothly, "Sure, babe, but we knew you

wouldn't be doing nothin' wrong." The girl sat silent, trying to digest that one.

Eddy leaned on the short counter and said, "Tell the boss there's an old roommate of his out here. Tell him it was a little room."

The girl didn't move. Eddy lifted his head and now there was menace in his tone. "Get moving," he rapped. "Go on!"

She jumped at that, but recovered her poise before she reached the inner door and snapped, "I don't get it. I hope the boss drops you down a hole, shouting like that." She went in grumbling, came out almost immediately. There was a fat, bald-headed little man in shirtsleeves behind her. He was smoking a cigar. His face fell when he saw Eddy and the boys.

Eddy gave him a paw. "'Lo, Dim. H'ya?"

Marty Dimenza took the cigar out of his mouth like it had suddenly tasted not so good. "'Lo, Eddy. H'ya?" he said mechanically. He was watching the other boys, particularly Bright. Bright was looking at the girl, beginning to go over to her.

Eddy said, "I got some ideas on shipping business, Dim. Maybe we can talk 'em over private, uh?" That was for the benefit of the girl, and Marty Dimenza caught on.

"Sure, sure," he said. "Come on in." Then he hesitated. "I ain't but two chairs and not much room. Maybe your friends'll wait out here while we talk?"

Gino said, "Sure," for the boys, and just at that moment Bright did something quick to the girl and she gasped and jumped away, her face flaming mad.

She went for her hat and said, "If these apes stay, I go. What the hell do you think I am, for this buzz-head to maul?"

Eddy said, quickly, "She don't leave." Because a girl like that might go out and open her mouth. The girl started to argue, but Eddy said. "Okay, okay. We'll take Bright in with us, then he won't get in your hair, babe."

Dimenza waddled back into his office saying, "Make any arrangements you like, I don't mind. I'm only the boss." But he was wary, uncertain. When the door closed on the others he said, "You're in jake, huh? Come clean, what're ya up to?"

Eddy jeered, "Now, that sounds nice and friendly, Dim. You ain't changed, not one bit. Just the same big, open-hearted Marty Dimenza. *State Convict No. DW1444.*"

Dimenza didn't alter his expression. He said, "That doesn't answer my questions." His eyes were on the sack that Eddy had brought in. "You wouldn't have looked me up just to tell me that, so I guess trouble's brought you here. What trouble? That's all I ask."

Eddy put his feet up on the desk. Bright found a magazine and started looking for pretty girls. Eddy said, "We were passing. We thought we'd drop in. Yeah, suppose we are in trouble? All we want is to lie up until it's safe for us to take the road back to New York."

Dim asked the obvious question. "Why don't you

take it right now?"

"Cops," answered Eddy laconically. "They got the roads watched. Maybe they'll stop watching when they get tired."

"Cops don't tire easily. Not always. Depends what you've done." Dim's eyes narrowed in his fat face. "I told you to come clean. I want to know what's back of all this before I do anything to help you—and what cut do I get, anyway?"

So Eddy told him. "We came to Freshwater last week. We cased a bank just outside town, and this afternoon we stuck it up."

Dimenza's eyes looked again at the sack and now they had a warmer feeling. "A bank?" Then he seemed surprised. "I didn't hear of no bank being knocked off?"

"The cops heard. We ran slap into a roadblock less than five minutes after leaving the bank. We had to double back into town to get away from 'em."

"A roadblock?" Dimenza was thinking, hard.

Eddy got to his feet and began pacing the little office. His face was savage. "Jesus Christ, how they got to know so soon, I just don't imagine. We reckoned on a clear ten- or twelve-hour lead. Then we go right into the arms of a posse almost round the first corner." For a moment he stood still, the better to curse.

Dimenza's eyes were back on that sack, greedily estimating. After a while he said, "You got a tough break, pardner. You should've picked another day." Eddy turned to look at him. "That posse you ran into, it wasn't looking for you at all."

"No?"

"No. Maybe if you'd have driven quietly up to it they might have let you through." Dim paused, his eyes now never leaving that sack. "It's someone else the cops are after. They've got Pretty Boy trapped in Freshwater."

Eddy said, "Pretty Boy?" not understanding. "I don't get it. Who's this Pretty Boy fellar, anyway? What's his racket?"

"He just kills people. Dames. Nastily." Dim was terse. "Well, he's done for one dame, anyway. Don't you read the papers?"

Eddy snapped his lingers. He was beginning to remember now. "*Him*," he said. "The guy they call the Sex Murderer. They were looking for him, uh?" His eyes were mad as hell, thinking of the bad break that had come to them. Then he saw that Dimenza's greedy gaze was on the sack in the chair. He cooled down and started to think.

First thing he decided was that there was no need to tell his former cellmate in Indiana State Jail about the shooting of the cop. Maybe the fellow wasn't so badly hurt, anyway.

He said, "We're in hot with the cops, anyway. We had to ram a cop can before we got away. Now they'll be looking for us."

Dim said, "What do you want from me?"

Eddy sat on the desk and swung his yellow shoes. "We want to lie low here until after dark. Then we want a car and someone to show us the backways out of Freshwater County. We'll pay well."

Dim said, "Like hell you will. There's something you guys don't know. They've got a Vigilance Committee in Freshwater. They got tired of being run by cops in the pay of racketeers and politicos, and a couple of weeks ago they surprised everyone by coming out with a Vigilance Committee. They've round about a coupla hundred in it now, and pretty mean they are, too. They're out to clean up Freshwater, they say, though Boss Myrtle's got his own ideas on that subject."

Eddy said, "You got the nicest voice. Now tell me, what in hell it all adds up to?"

Dim kept looking at that sack. He said, "It adds up to your being trapped here in Freshwater on account of some woman was murdered two-three days back in New York. They got the Vigilantes out watching all the back roads, and by now I guess they'll be looking for five gunnies as well as Pretty Boy. You fixed yourself in a nice place, brother." He was sarcastic.

Eddy said, "The hell we have," aghast. He looked down at his yellow toes for a moment and then said, shrewdly, "You got any ideas, Dim?"

Dim said, "I could have, if you had dough—big dough."

"Like?"

"Like ten grand, say."

Eddy thought for a moment. "Maybe we could ante up with that amount if we knew we were getting outa this place in one piece." That would leave about ten grand left and that wasn't peanuts.

Dim rose. He couldn't keep his eyes off that sack and he ran a wet little tongue over fat lips as he thought of his share of it. The way he was planning, there'd be a grand in it for himself for certain: and a grand took some picking up these days.

He said, "I'm gonna fix things for you. The price is ten grand. Okay?"

Eddy said, reluctantly, "Okay." Then: "How're you aimin' to do it?" There was suspicion in his tone. He had never believed in the tag that there was honour among thieves, and Marty Dimenza was a double-crosser if ever there was one. But he might play straight for a cut in the bankroll.

Dim reached into a cupboard for his hat and coat. The mops and cleaning things were in the same cupboard—it was that kind of an office that Freshwater Shippers Inc. had. He wiped off the dust and stuck his hat on.

"I'm off to see Boss Myrtle. If anyone can fix this, Boss can. He runs this town—cops and all. He'll do most anything for ten grand."

Then he went out. Eddy went out after him and got the boys in a corner away from the girl and told them what he had arranged. Gino got mad at the thought of losing ten grand, but then he was always greedy. Maxie Christman just shrugged his thin shoulders and said, "That's how it is, Gino. We got no option but to play ball—at Dimenza's price."

He lit up from a butt. They had all been smoking hard and the room was foul with tobacco fumes. The girl was sitting sullenly by the window that looked across the warehouse roofs along by the harbour wall. When Bright came leering vacuously into the room, she took fright and reached for a heavy paper punch, but Eddy sent him back into the boss's office out of the way and she subsided.

Then they sat down to wait. They were nervous, because nobody trusted an ex-con like Marty Dimenza. Boy Fehse took a chair and sat right behind the door in case of surprise, and this time no one told him to keep his hand away from his shoulder holster.

Half an hour later they heard someone in the passage outside. Then the door began to open. Dimenza waddled in. Nobody relaxed until he was right inside the room and they saw that no one was following. As the door closed, everyone sighed. The girl was watching, not missing a thing.

Dim said, "I hope you got the dough, because I've fixed it."

Eddy looked at Maxie. He could trust that guy— almost. He said, "You sit out here and keep the dame company, Max. This time we'll all go inside and have a talk."

Inside, Dim said there was nothing to talk about until he'd seen ten grand. He seemed nervous, his fingers clenching and unclenching as though in anticipation of something pleasant between them.

Eddy growled. "We might as well count up, then."

They did. They were disappointed. In all they had only pulled in around sixteen thousand dollars. They tried to argue Marty Dimenza out of a few grand, but he knew he had them where he wanted them and he held out and in the end ten grand lay before him.

Then he told the news. "I fixed it with the boss," he said and he was lying. "For ten grand the boss is willing to pull out the Vigilantes from the back rounds, so's you can get through on a dirt track as far as Mason County and the New York state highway."

"Yeah," said Gino. "And how do we get there?"

Dimenza said, "I'm gonna take you in my own car, personal like. Me, I know the way better'n anybody." He was boasting, and some inner excitement shook his voice. Eddy was watching narrowly.

He looked at his companions. Gino seemed satisfied. "If the guy's comin' along, guess it seems on the level."

Eddy nodded towards the piles of dollar bills, reluctantly, grudgingly, and Dim at once scooped them up into a soapbox along with the mops and brushes.

He said, "When we go, that stays here. That's fair, ain't it?" He didn't trust these New York gunnies. Somehow you don't trust anyone when you're pulling a fast one yourself.

And Marty Dimenza was certainly doing that. He had never been near the big boss, Racketeer Myrtle.

CHAPTER FIVE
BOSS MYRTLE
INTERVENES

Lanny didn't get away with it. He came down to the pier head and went across to speak to the police car there. The sergeant in charge reported no sign of Pretty Boy.

"And the ship pulls out in twenty minutes," Lanny said, looking at his watch and then up at the swank coast cruiser. "Then that'll be one less exit to watch."

The sergeant said, "We got a description of the five gunnies who did for Kippax. That's their car up the hill there." He was watching Lanny closely. Lanny thought humorously that that was getting to be a habit with police sergeants.

"You were about to say something, sergeant?" said Lanny politely. He was bigger than the sergeant—almost the biggest man in the Freshwater force—and that gave him an advantage. Somehow a big man is intimidating when it comes to cross-talk.

The sergeant said, quickly, "Sure. It's nothing—sir. Just wondered if you'd got the recall message from HQ five minutes ago."

Lanny knew it was no good bluffing; that would only lead to the sergeant relaying the message to him. So he said, "I got it, and I don't intend to do a damn' thing about it. And you can report that if you like back at HQ."

At which moment Lieutenant Murdoch came down the hill on a motorcycle. He was young, slick, coldly unemotional. If the police chief was in Boss Myrtle's pocket, then Murdoch was in alongside him, too.

Lanny waited, his face hard and unsmiling. Murdoch shoved back his visor and said, "You didn't acknowledge a message sent out to you a few minutes ago, captain. So I came to find you."

"Well?"

"You don't need to go back to HQ now," said Murdoch coolly. "You don't need to go anywhere. In fact you'd better go home, because there's a message back at HQ that someone's there to see you."

But Lanny was waiting for the important part of the message to come out.

"Go on," he said gently. "Give me the works."

Murdoch started up his motorcycle, and looked round to see that the way was clear for him to pull out.

"The works? Oh, yes. The chief guessed you might forget to do anything about the Vigilantes, so he gave the order for them to return home himself. The chief doesn't like amateurs interfering in police matters."

"Maybe," said Lanny grimly. "Maybe, though, it's someone else giving these orders, someone who doesn't like opposition in this town. Someone named

Boss Myrtle, who runs the police force, the town, and all the rackets connected with Freshwater."

Murdoch kicked in the gear and said, "You wanna sew up your lip. You're in enough trouble with your tongue already. If you were a smart cop you could be doing well, with that captain's uniform." With that he let out the clutch and roared away.

Lanny said, viciously, "Someday I'll bounce my fist so hard on his sleek head he'll have a permanent wave for the rest of his life—if he lives!" Then he went slowly back to his car, thinking.

For Lanny knew he was up against it. Knew that the Myrtle Machine had moved in against him. That order, to get off the job, could mean only one thing—he was being retired.

So, because he was built like that, Lanny told his driver to take him back to HQ. If they wanted a fight, he would meet them more than halfway.

The sun was throwing long shadows now, but it was still pleasantly hot and there was an exhilarating atmosphere about the late-spring afternoon. Suddenly Lanny didn't feel balled up and savage any more. Maybe it was the sunshine, maybe the fact that he knew now where he stood...maybe it was the prospect of an out-and-out fight coming along any minute now.

Lanny had wanted a fight for weeks past. Now he could see one just ahead, and it did him good.

He got in some preliminary sparring even before he entered the HQ. As he came straightening out of the police car in the big, concrete yard, he saw two familiar cars. Boss Myrtle's. Half a dozen apes were fraternising with the cops on duty in the park.

Lanny strode across to where they lounged against the wings of the big, fast, expensive sedans. He said, bitingly, "You, you scum, get to hell off this police park and take your buggies with you!"

They stiffened but didn't move. Lanny turned on the cop.

"And you, what in Hades are you up to, letting these ape inside here? Run 'em out, fer Crissakes. They stink!"

The apes came up snarling at that. They took it for being offensive. Lanny stood and watched them, a tight grin oh his face. He wasn't scared of Boss Myrtle's strong-arm men.

The cop came out with the name. He said, sullenly, defensively, "It's Boss Myrtle. He just drove in."

Lanny roared, "The hell with Boss Myrtle! How long's that crap been running the Force? Get 'em out of here, I tell you."

One of the hoods had his hand in his pocket. They were flat-faced, leather-cheeked, sallow, these apes. They were all different, and yet they all looked alike. Just a bunch of no good, two-timing ex-New York hoods.

Lanny walked up to the hood. He said, "I'll kick that hand outa your pocket if you don't get it out quick." He stood, poised ready. The gunnie was intimidated and came out with the hand—quick. Then Lanny embraced them all with a biting glare. "You got ten seconds. After that I'll slam you behind bars if you're still around. Get moving!"

They moved. Plainly they were bewildered and didn't know what to do. They were followers, not leaders, for their boss didn't happen to be around just then to think for them. They got into their cars and reversed out of the yard savagely, to pull up on the public parking lot round the corner.

Lanny felt better after that. He went up to the desk. The sergeant was answering a telephone call. He said, "Okay, lady.... Sure, we'll do that. But you got nothing to worry about. Maybe he's shootin' crap some place with the boys.... He don't shoot crap? Then he's a mighty fine husband, lady, and you got cause to worry! Okay, okay, we'll let you know if anything comes through."

He replaced the receiver. He had a flat face and there was the map of Ireland on it. He yapped, "Some dame ain't seen her husband for a coupla hours an' she gets worried! You wouldn't believe," he said, then turned to write a name down.

Lanny said, "These hoods that are tearing round the burg. You got anything on them yet, sergeant? Any reports through of a big job being pulled in Freshwater?"

The sergeant laboriously blotted his book and said, "Not a thing, captain. Freshwater's just as Freshwater always is—deader than the mussels under the pier... and just as smelly."

Lanny went up. He didn't hurry, though that wasn't because he was scared now—he found he was thinking, working up a few strong cards.... They weren't many.

When he went into the chief's room, he found Alastair Myrtle and Boss there, and Boss Myrtle was also doing some phoning. You'd have thought he was the president, the way the chief shushed for silence while Boss ended his message. Lanny, uninvited, draped his long legs around a chair and tossed a cigarette expertly into his mouth. The chief glared. Lanny flicked his match on to the thick pile carpet just for the hell of the thing.

Boss Myrtle was saying, "Keep looking. I don't want her anywhere near town today, not with this Pretty Boy killer roaming the streets.... Sure, I know all that, lightning doesn't strike twice—they don't make a habit of these kind of killings.... But get that girl back home and keep an eye on her! Get off your fanny and find her!"

That was a command. Lanny thought: Bet they're spraining ankles to try and find the boss's daughter pronto, and not for the first time he wondered at a crook like Myrtle having a daughter like Bonnie. He remembered the old saying, about the fairest flowers blossoming on a dung heap....

Boss Myrtle had recovered by the time he turned round. He was like his brother, only heavier, more stooped, older, and without that military moustache. And harder.

Alastair was smiling affably, with all his usual good humour, at Lanny, but Boss Myrtle merely looked at him coldly, with menace in his deep-set eyes.

The chief kept looking at Boss Myrtle, as if seeking

a lead. He flannelled, "I sent for you, captain. There are things I have to say to you." Lanny said, "Sure, and I know what they are. And it's unusual to say them to a subordinate in the presence of people like Boss Myrtle and his brother." His eyes were mocking, and it made the chief uneasy. Lanny Just had always been a tough man to handle, and he knew this wasn't going to be easy.

His eyes flickered again to Boss Myrtle; he cleared his throat, and grated, harshly, "You got only yourself to blame, captain. I can't have officers taking it on themselves to ignore my orders. I'm suspending you from duty until such a time as I have chance to consider your case."

"Which means," said Lanny softly, "you're easing me out of the Force right now, huh?" He turned on the massive Boss Myrtle. "That's how you want it, isn't it? You've got no time for cops who won't take your orders. So you've turned the heat on the chief and made him shove me out."

The chief went through the motions of working up an anger. He said, "You be careful, captain. That's a slander uttered in the presence of witnesses. I could take your pants down for that...."

Lanny said, easily. "If you like I'll get it printed in the local paper. Then you can roast me for libel...." Suddenly he stopped bantering. His grey eyes held such contempt they scorched. He grated, "What kind of a chief are you, to take orders from dirty, chiselling crooks like the Myrtles?"

The Myrtles said nothing, so it was left to the chief. He came back after a pause with—"I don't take orders from no one."

"Yeah? It was your idea to pull the Vigilantes out, huh? Like hell it was! Boss Myrtle's back of that order. This new Vigilance Committee's a menace to his reign as King Crook of Freshwater, and he's out to crush it. It's Boss Myrtle calling them in, and my guess is he'll try and stop them from ever getting together again." He leaned forward, accusingly, "I'm right, aren't I? Boss Myrtle's already told you to bust up the Vigilantes, hasn't he?"

The chief licked his lips. He was an old man and at his time of life he didn't like these shindigs. The worst of it was he had no case and knew it, and he didn't like batting on the defensive.

He tried to sound detached and magisterial, but it came over weak.

"Mr. Myrtle and his brother are citizens of Freshwater. They are taxpayers, and as such they have every right to express a point of view. They and a number of well-known businessmen—"

"Name 'em?" said Lanny cuttingly.

It threw the chief out of his stride for a moment. He tried to bluster. "I'll give you their names when I'm ready. There are quite a few of them." He glanced quickly at the silent Boss Myrtle. "They don't like this new-formed Vigilance Committee, and they have appealed to me to suspend it. I have agreed to do so until such a time as we can discuss the matter in detail."

The stilted way of speaking wasn't lost on Lanny. He began to get the hang of it....

Lanny scoffed. "Like me, that means the Vigilantes are on their way out!" Somewhere outside a lot of noise had begun, men shouting, horns blasting. They took no notice of it for the moment.

Lanny said, "What is there to discuss, anyway? What's wrong with good, honest citizens banding to form a Vigilance Committee? Vigilantes are as old as the United States—older. They come together when they think there's need for law and order in a community."

"Haven't we got law and order in Freshwater?" The chief tried to fight back. "What's this uniform signify?"

Lanny let his eyes trail over the smooth, smiling Alastair and the icy-cold, stoop-shouldered Boss. He said, "Maybe you can tell him, Boss. It doesn't amount to much, does it?"

Boss Myrtle stirred at that. He wasn't used to hearing other people talk so much. His voice came grinding up from the depths, and when the words emerged they clattered like rusty iron bolts dropping into a bucket.

"You talk a lot, captain. You'd do better to keep your mouth shut and your ears open. I'm not going to have armed men going around Freshwater, no matter what their excuse." Boss Myrtle didn't go in for subtleties; he was the boss, and he told them straight what was in his mind.

Lanny said, "Only a few are armed, and they are only sporting-guns and the fellows have licences for them."

The chief said, "I've called in all licences. No one's gonna carry a weapon in Freshwater until I've had a chance to look into this matter."

"No one?" said Lanny softly. He rose slowly from his chair. That blue captain's uniform made him look very big. Alastair wasn't ready. Lanny exulted, because he had been busting to wipe that slow smile off the racketeer's face.

Alastair was big but he came up out of his chair fast. He found himself slammed hard against the chief's desk, hurting the small of his back. Lanny dived his hand under Alastair's armpit and came out with a Harrington and Richardson .38 calibre revolver.

He tossed it on to the chief's desk. "He won't need this, then," he said. He was smiling; it was good to lay hands on someone like Alastair Myrtle.

It was a satisfactory though meaningless gesture. They all knew that the moment Lanny went out of the room, Alastair would get his gun back.

The noise outside was getting deafening. Alastair stood up, slowly rubbing his back. Lanny had to hand it to him; that slow, good-humoured smile was already back on his face.

Alastair said, so nicely, "You can get them to start chipping in a date on your tombstone, captain. It'll be 1951."

Lanny said, "Maybe, but I wasn't born yesterday." He was across by the window, looking down. An angry mob of men had driven up to the main entrance.

There must have been at least a hundred, and they were waving sticks and a few had sporting-guns. They had come by car, and while there were a few up-to-date vehicles in the bunch, most looked worn and old and not so prosperous.

Few tradesmen had been prosperous since Boss Myrtle and his hoods came to settle in Freshwater.

Lanny said, "The Vigilance Committee don't seem to approve of being told to disband and go back home."

The chief felt that here was one situation he could handle.

He looked down at the mob, then rang through to the desk.

"Take their guns away and slap 'em in jail, if they don't disperse immediately," he ordered. He came back grumbling,

"What the hell, what kind of a town is this where armed mobs go around telling the police what to do?" And that was good, with Boss Myrtle sitting there.

Lanny said, "You know what you're doing, chief, don't you? There's a man in this town, a particularly brutal murderer. He was trapped while we had the Vigilantes helping the police to watch all roads out. Probably we could have closed in on him and picked him up—and maybe also picked up the gunnies who shot Patrolman Kippax.

"But you've just opened up a lot of ways for them all to escape. You don't give a damn if they do get away, so long as you break this Vigilance Committee!"

Boss Myrtle said, harshly, "You've got enough cops

to pick 'em all up. What for do you want the help of that rabble, anyway?"

Lanny faced him. He went on to a new subject. "You've got a daughter, Boss. She's a nice girl. I know she's a nice girl because I've seen quite a lot of her lately."

Boss's eyes came up at that, startled. Lanny nodded grimly. "Yeah, I know what's in your mind. But I haven't run after her—not with you as her father and me a cop. But we just can't seem to help running into each other in this little burg."

Words clattered from Boss Myrtle's mouth. "What's my daughter got to do with these Vigilantes, captain? And just pick your words carefully when you talk about Bonnie, be warned!"

They were standing now, only a yard separating them two big, strong men, facing each other with eyes that seemed to be battling.

Lanny knew he had him on the raw, and his voice was merciless as he pressed home his advantage. "Just think, Boss. You think the world of your daughter, big-time crook though you are. She's the only person in the world you have love and affection for—yeah?"

Boss Myrtle didn't say anything. But his eyes dared Lanny to say anything wrong against his daughter.

Now Lanny's voice was softer. "So, just think how you'd feel if anything happened to her *because you had forced the chief to withdraw the Vigilantes*!"

"I am thinking," grated Boss, "and I ain't worrying."

"No," blazed Lanny. "But there are six dangerous

men cooped up in this town, and if they're not picked up quickly they might do harm to some inoffensive person—maybe somebody else's daughter."

Boss Myrtle just shrugged. "They just got to look after themselves, that's all," he said indifferently. Lanny knew it was hopeless, that line of reasoning with the big boss. He sighed and walked across to the door. There he paused and said, "I just hope it's you that gets hurt, Boss. Badly. So they have to fit you with a wooden suit. You know why? Because then I'd go right ahead and marry Bonnie!"

He saw fury come into the eyes of the racketeer, but he wasn't waiting for any more words with Boss Myrtle and he slammed out.

He went straight into the radio room. A patrolman was removing a wire spool from the recording machine. He was only a fresh-faced kid from college, and he looked startled when he saw Lanny striding across.

Lanny said, "All that talk with the chief and the Myrtle's went down on record, didn't it?"

The patrolman nodded uncertainly. "The chief said it had to be recorded and for me to take the spool up to him afterward."

"Yeah." Lanny nodded. "I guessed so. The chief took care not to say a thing out of place. That gave me the idea our talk was going on record. I guess, properly edited, they could make that record talk against me."

The patrolman nodded. He said, "But I can't give you the spool, if that's what you're thinking, captain."

"I wouldn't ask you." Lanny smiled. This was his

fight and he couldn't get a new kid into trouble with him. He turned away. The young patrolman came in step beside him. Lanny suddenly realised that the light in the kid's eyes was hero worship. He'd seen it before, especially when he was playing football and an up and coming star.

The kid said, quickly, "Look, captain, we all know they're making trouble for you, and a lot of us don't like it. But—"

"But you just got to sit on the benches and watch, huh?" Lanny smiled and patted the youngster on his shoulder. It was a pretty strong young shoulder at that. "I know how it is. And thanks for your concern."

The young cop said, "You'd be surprised how many cops are fed up with this racket and would support you if you tried to bust it."

Lanny looked at him. He hadn't thought of that, hadn't thought that maybe a lot of cops here were sick of things and wanted to get them sorted out. "That sounds like an invitation to mutiny," he cracked back. "But maybe we'll leave that as a last resource. Maybe I can crack this affair open myself." Though as yet he hadn't much idea.

So he started to walk on again, and then the young patrolman stopped him. "There was something came over the tape after you'd left the room."

Lanny stared, waiting. The young cop went on.

"Boss Myrtle said, 'That's a job for you, Al. You know what to do'." The kid looked anxiously at Lanny, as if not wishing to be misinterpreted. "Of course, it could mean anything, but I think—"

"You think the boss has told his brother to get me rubbed out?" He looked at the spool. "And even that doesn't mean anything, not if it's played back to a rigged judge and jury."

Lanny looked at that spool again. It had doubtful value to him but it could possibly be edited to talk against him.

He knew, though, he couldn't get it from the patrolman short of clipping the kid under the jaw, and that was no way to keep friends.

He said cautiously, "You don't need to take it up right now, do you?" If it were left lying around the place for a while, he might have a chance to come back and get it.

Maybe the kid understood and really wanted to help him.

"Sure I don't need to take it for a while." Very deliberately he put it on a shelf. "Maybe not for an hour or so."

Lanny grinned. That kid was trying to help him. It did his heart good, the way one after another these cops were coming up and showing they were with him in this affair.

He let his eyes trail from the spool, nodded with satisfaction and left the young cop.

He went out and down the corridor. At the main entrance he paused. Alastair Myrtle had come down before him and was talking to his apes by the cars. One must have said something, for at once they all turned and looked at Lanny, their hands going into their pockets or under their arms.

Then they stood and waited for Lanny to come out of the building.

CHAPTER SIX
PRETTY BOY

Haim Joannou came slowly down the approach to the Freshwater promenade, at peace with the world. The sun was shining, the waves danced and sparkled, surf creamed in hissing long rollers up the hot, golden sands—there were people on the beach, laughing and playing, or lying contentedly under gaily-striped umbrellas. Back of them all were the long, open, balconied restaurants, suggesting pleasant coolness and even cooler drinks.

This, thought Haim, was better than New York. He was glad he had picked on Freshwater. Someone in the queue in New York had said, "Freshwater," and until then he hadn't even thought where he was going. So when it came his turn he had said, "Freshwater," too. And here he was.

He was in a good mood. He'd bought cigarettes at the station, and was assured that his charm hadn't been dissipated by the last days of threat and anxiety. The only trouble was the irritation on his neck. He thought the scratches were getting inflamed and might turn nasty.

He walked round the town for a while, just one more vacationer, whiling away a pleasant afternoon. Then he found his feet taking him into the old town, where the harbour was.

The sun was getting to be unpleasant on his unprotected neck, and he decided to get some medicated plaster for it. He was turning into a store when a man with yellow shoes came hurriedly from a side turning and bumped into him.

Haim said, politely, "I beg your pardon," though it wasn't his fault. But then he was habitually well-mannered, and a credit to his Greek father and mother who had spoilt him in his younger life. And it wasn't put on, that educated British accent; Haim Joannou had made a grand tour of Europe straight after leaving college. A woman just old enough to be his mother had paid for that tour. She hadn't wanted to, but Haim had told her what could happen if she didn't pay up. It was blackmail, and she had a husband.

He wasn't so nice as he looked, Haim Joannou.

The girl inside the shop, charming as all girls are when they wear white, new-laundered coats, showed that she thought him swell, anyway. Her eyes took on that quick glint of interest that came to every female when they looked on the Greek god-like Joannou. And the dark, wavy-haired handsome Adonis turned on the tap of charm as he always did when in the presence of a woman.

For women were his business, his livelihood. Haim Joannou of the film star profile had long ago decided that while there was a woman left in the world he need not starve.

He looked from brown, sparkling eyes at the white-coated girl, waiting expectantly across the array of drugs and chemist's sundries, and suddenly he felt that curious disturbing sensation creeping up his spine. It made his whole body tingle...it was something that seemed to have grown on him increasingly in the past few years, a thrill that lightened his muscles and made his mouth grow dry in anticipation.

It had partially manifested itself a few times in the past, and the consequences had been for a time a trifle worrying. But the victims, women, had been well-picked and just ran away from him afterwards and said nothing to anyone.

Only, one hadn't been able to run away. And that had been the biggest thrill of all....

Maxie Christman, Boy Fehse, Bright, and Gino Lucci went past the store at that moment. It was the nearest they ever got to the man who would bring them soon to their deaths, yet they never knew it and passed on to meet Marty Dimenza....

Joannou's rich, vibrant voice said, "I want some medicated plaster. I have a scratch on my neck.... Perhaps you could fit it on for me?" That honey European accent had always softened the dames.

The girl let her eyes drop, so that he would not see the pleasure in them. She could and certainly would administer first aid. She did. And her hands felt soft and cool when they pressed gently around the inflamed parts.

She smiled when she had finished. "I guess your girlfriend took a dislike to you," she said, and there was the old glint of jealousy in her eyes that comes to every daughter of Eve when she thinks of a rival for a desirable man.

Joannou knew the value of the unexpected, said, softly, "Yes, she's jealous...my cat." and saw the pleasure flood back into the girl's eyes. Nineteen or ninety, they wanted all men for themselves. Well, that could be turned to advantage by a smart man.

He said goodbye, lingering as if he found her company satisfactory. You never knew when being liked by a woman mightn't come in useful. It made her feel good, and there were stars in her eyes as she watched him go out into the sunshine.

A kid came up with a special edition and tried to sell it to him. Joannou smiled and shook his head. Since those first editions he hadn't wanted to read a newspaper. He was safe enough and he didn't like what was being said about him.

That's finished with, he thought. I'm on holiday and all that's over and done with.

But it had given him a shock, that business. It hadn't been planned—just something...that curious, mounting thrill...and he'd found himself doing it. And liking it, loving it, enjoying that fever-hot thrill while it lasted. And it hadn't lasted long enough.

But never again. It was too dangerous. He'd got away with it this once, but a second time....

A police car came down the street, loudspeaker talking to them. Joannou wasn't listening, because he didn't feel it could interest him. He was heading for the busy part of the harbour, where the fishing vessels were coming in.

He bumped into a woman who had abruptly stopped, then realised that most people had stopped all along that crowded sidewalk. They were watching that police car, listening so as not to miss what was being broadcast from the loudspeakers.

Haim Joannou suddenly realised the intense excitement that pervaded the street at that moment, and abruptly jerked his thoughts from the past and tried to hear what was being said by the police. He got one word, the last. It sounded like "...papers." He saw that the kid with the papers was doing a roaring trade and he was tempted to go and buy one, but the crush was too great around the boy and he decided not to bother.

All the same he found himself interested, and wondering what had got Freshwater worked up so. It couldn't be a ball game, because cops surely wouldn't be using their loudspeakers for such a subject....

He walked on, came to the galvanised railings where the wall lifted above the broad, warm beach, and stood against them, revelling as the pleasant breeze rippled his black, wavy hair. Sure, this was the life. Maybe he'd do well to stay in Freshwater; New York was no place for him now. Yeah, Freshwater—he'd find some lonely, older woman (women older than himself always fell harder—and quicker) and maybe stay around the place for the rest of the summer. He didn't think it would be hard lo arrange.

Down below a smart young brunette in a bikini came high-stepping through the uneven yellow sand. She was carrying a newspaper. She sprawled face down just below him, and she made a good picture with only her button of a red bottom costumed. She was reading, Joannou could see over her shoulder, could see pictures, but couldn't make out what they were.

The police car was riding round again. Now he heard it, the tail end of what was being said, anyway. "Get a newspaper. Co-operate with the police, *and keep your eyes open!*"

And Joannou was already turning, already deciding to buy a newspaper. Because he had seen two words headlining up from the newspaper below.

A kid came rushing down with an armful of papers. He was so excited no one could understand what he was bawling. And Joannou got it again, that excitement that permeated the atmosphere of Freshwater. He wondered why he hadn't felt it before, and wished he had and had done something about it.

He reached over the quick-forming throng and got a paper. Then he went back to the railings and faced out to sea while he unfolded the sheet.

And a little gasp came from him...shocked horror. For he read, "MANIAC MURDERER," and underneath looked onto a picture of himself.

CHAPTER SEVEN
G-MEN

Lanny looked down the steps towards the bright sunshine, looked at those curiously tense figures by the powerful Myrtle auto, and his head came up in an abrupt, pugnacious gesture.

Under his breath he growled, "You crap! You think I'm so easy?"

Because he wasn't easy. He wasn't such a dumb cluck as to go out to his own jalopy and get run off the highway at some quiet spot, say, where the railroad crossed a waste lot just by his apartment block. The Myrtle mob could get away with anything, even murder, given the slightest opportunity to commit the deed.

Only Lanny didn't figure on being a corpse that quick.

He thought: You've left it too late. He glanced at his watch and wondered how long it would take a fast car to get over from Mason County. He guessed it should be here any time now. That was one of the cards he had been mentally holding for the last half hour, the card the chief should have remembered.

He went back to the desk, because that was as good a place as any to be for the next few minutes. The desk sergeant was just replacing the phone.

"You wouldn't believe," he yapped. "Another dame misplaces her husband a coupla hours and gets worried. Now, my wife...."

Lanny was looking out through the big, open doors. There was a fast-moving car approaching along the Western Highway. He thought: This could be it.

The sergeant had carefully put on some glasses and now, head tilted back, was reading a new edition that had just come in. He was a crude, fleshy old man. He licked his lips, and yapped again, "The things that Pretty Boy fellar did to her. You wouldn't believe, would you, cap'n?"

Lanny said, shortly, he would. That car was slowing. Could be it was going to turn into the park.

The sergeant leaned forward confidentially eyes blinking over the top of his glasses. "I seen the all-stations report," he said. "Not the one they give the Press—that's kid stuff. You know, the details." Again he licked his fat lips, the old sinner. "The things he did. Taped her mouth, then tied her across that hotel bed. And the things he did until she died. You wouldn't believe." He was monotonous.

The car *was* turning in. Lanny knew it was the one he had been reckoning on, and now he turned and looked at the old man behind the desk and there was loathing in his glance.

He was wondering if contact with crime and brutality

would turn him the same way, would make him hardened and callous. He hoped to God it wouldn't!

He moved a couple of yards away from the desk, because he didn't want to hear that yapping voice on that subject.

He thought: He likes it. Likes every detail. It's better than the movies for him. A woman had to die like that, horribly, just so as to please him and millions of other sensation-seekers.

They didn't think—didn't try to put themselves into that poor woman's place as she lay helpless on the hotel bed and died, because there are limits to what a woman can stand. And what that killer had done....

And she hadn't been a woman, really; she'd just followed a woman's calling. They didn't know her real name, didn't know her age or where she came from. But she couldn't have been twenty, the reports said. A kid—and to die like that.

And in dying make a feast for old men like the desk sergeant.

Four bulky young men had got out of the car. They looked at Myrtle's apes as they passed, then started to mount the steps.

The sergeant lifted his voice to reach him, and it was professionally admiring.

"You gotta hand it to the city cops. Guess they were right smart. A fellar brings a dame into an hotel, books a room for Mr. and Mrs. Smith. Next morning Mr. Smith has gone, and his wife for a night's lyin' there pretty dead.

"You wouldn't think, among six million people, they'd ever get a lead on 'Mr. Smith,' now would you? But they did—within a day.

"Some cop there sits back and uses his brains. He says 'Godamnit, every time I take the missus out there's a fellar shovin' a card into my hand and sayin' I've been photographed. Maybe that happened to Mr. Smith when he walked that time up to that hotel—if he walked.'

"And the Smith pair did walk, and it was so. They got every street photographer in the area roped in, got their pictures and developed 'em, and then they sat the hotel staff down in front of the pile and said, 'Find the lady—and her killer'!"

The four hulky men were coming into the office. Coming straight across to where Lanny stood. The sergeant's voice was droning on.

"They found a picture, all right. The girl and the fellar. Bet he never knew he had been photographed. Suddenly a girl squawks. 'That's him. I knew him at once, he was such a pretty boy.' So, captain, that's how the newspapers came to christen him Pretty Boy."

Lanny walked towards the men, out of earshot of the desk-sergeant. The sergeant had suddenly stopped talking however. He had been dotting the I's and crossing the T's of his last entry, and now something struck him and he was looking in surprise at what he had written.

Lanny said, "Can I help you?"

One of the men showed a leather-cased identification card. His photograph was on it. Lanny grinned and said, "F.B.I. I knew it the moment I saw you glim those apes outside."

He introduced himself. The G-men relaxed and became affable. They were typical Hoover men, hand-picked out of America's millions, young graduates with degrees in law and thick muscle on the backs of their necks. That was the type of man Hoover had recruited to war on crime in America. Bright, intelligent young men with legal qualifications. F.B.I. training had put the muscle on their necks.

Lanny said, "I'm Captain Just, head of the Freshwater Detective Division." He didn't say he had been suspended from duty, didn't think it necessary. He wasn't going to be taken off the job all that easily, and he had no intention of resigning from it.

He told them about the shooting of the unfortunate patrolman by the gang of five in the later-abandoned Pontiac. There wasn't much to tell. He also mentioned that Pretty Boy was reported as being in town.

The G-man—Scheer, his name was—said, "Shooting a cop's a Federal offence; that's why we're here. Killing a dame's work only for the local police—your job, captain."

"Sure," said Lanny. "But as head of the division, my job's to liaise with you to find the gunnies, at the same time I must try to pull in Pretty Boy." And he had other ideas that embraced the usefulness of the G-man, and he wanted to pull them out at the appropriate time.

That was one thing the chief should have remembered when the Myrtles demanded his, Lanny's, removal. G-men were on their way to town, and G-men were above corruption, and Lanny was seeing a way to use them in his back-to-the-wall fight against the racketeers and the corrupt local police force. They would have been surprised, those G-men, if they'd known what was flitting through that big young police captain's mind right then!

G-man Scheer said, "We'd better go along to see the chief."

Lanny said, "He's in conference." He wanted the G-men to meet other people in the town first, like Vigilante Joe, who had started the fight back against the mobsters. There were Federal offences other than shooting cops, and he thought that, given time in Freshwater, these smart G-men would tumble to a thing or two on their own account. At the moment it was better he kept his own mouth shut: anything he said would be declared the malice of a discredited cop....

The sergeant saved the situation. He was still staring down at his ledger, and his face had the puzzled expression of a man who is seeing something and doesn't know whether to believe it.

He called, "Can I show you something, cap?"

Lanny thought: God, more dirt in the paper? But went across.

The sergeant was stubbing with a stiff forefinger at the writing in the ledger. He yapped, "I just noticed something, captain. Them two dames that misplaced their husbands. Both fellars work out at Green Hollow; both work in the same bank. Now, I'm wondering...."

He took off his glasses and rubbed round his eyes to ease the tautened skin. "I mean, bank fellars ain't like you and me. They're steady guys, they go home to their wives. Usually. But maybe these guys have got ideas on the bank money on their own account. I mean, two guys missing from the same bank...."

Lanny snapped alert. "Got it!" he rapped. "Isn't that what we've been waiting for, sergeant?" The G-men were close up on him, sensing that something was about to break in connection with their case.

Lanny thought: That Green Hollow bank. Would be East Coast Banking Corporation's branch. He looked at the names on the ledger, recognised them. Sure, it *was* that bank. Then he thought hard for a minute. He remembered a third bank employee up there, a Czech who had done well in the war. A resourceful guy who had figured in a police case and been very helpful. He was temporary manager now, Lanny thought.

It took him a moment to remember his name, then he got it and grabbed the telephone directory. Czanik, that was the name. He dialled, got through. A woman's voice.

"Is Mr. Czanik there? No?" Worry displaced the first gladness when she said "Hello" to him. "Do you know where he is?" He listened, then said, "Quit worrying; he'll be back soon. Mrs. Czanik," and then cut off without frightening her further with his identity.

He thought, turning: And he might not be back. If

it's a bank snatch. anything might have happened. Mrs. Czanik might be a widow now.

To the waiting G-men he rapped, "That's three of them, three sober, dependable guys who have failed to go home to their wives. *Bank employees*!"

The F.B.I. men were getting round to it. Lanny said, "We've been waiting for a report of some crime big enough to justify gunning a cop in an escape. My guess is—this is it, a bank stick-up. Let's get out there!"

He was about to go when he remembered something. Two things. He said, "Get in touch with the district manager of the East Coast Banking Corporation"—to the desk sergeant. "Tell him I want him out at their Green Hollow branch just as fast as he can get there. Don't tell him any more than that."

To the G-men he said, "I'll be with you in a minute. Go out and wait for me in your car."

He ducked back along the corridor, returned in a matter of a minute with something bulky in his pocket. When he came running down the steps out into the sunshine, he saw the group around the Myrtle car stiffen again, as their eyes fixed on him—hard. Alastair said something, and at once one of the men slipped behind the wheel and the others started to clamber in clumsily after him.

Lanny paused, his voice baiting. "You palookas, what do you think you're up to?"

Alastair was smiling. Lanny said, mockingly, "You got some ideas—bad ones. Just see if they're not!"

Then he got in beside the burly G-men.

They hadn't expected that, and their faces fell as the F.B.I. car picked up and then shot into life. Looking back, Lanny saw them conferring together, then saw the gang get out of the car again.

They'd called it off for the day....

* * * * * * *

The district bank manager turned out to be resident in Green Hollow himself, and he was outside the bank, examining the door, as they drove up.

Lanny strode across, suddenly recognising him. He said, "This is the F.B.I., Mr. Halladan. One of our men's been shot this afternoon by some gunnies. We think they might have been doing things to your branch here. You'll have duplicate keys?"

Halladan was startled, recovered, and nodded. "Sure," he said. "Shall we go in?"

Lanny nodded. Halladan opened the door and stood aside to let the police officers enter. Lanny took one look at the open drawers and unlocked cupboards, the bills and papers and small change on the long counter, and knew he was hot on the trail.

Halladan said, "This is all wrong," shocked to see one of his branches left like that after closing hours.

Lanny said, "That's what we thought." Then he and the G-men went quickly over the premises, searching, examining everything, trying to pick up a clue. There was little to see.

Then they had a conference, while Halladan sorted through the papers to see what he could find. Scheer said, "It could be a conspiracy: a walk-out with the bank's dough on the part of the staff." But he didn't seem to believe it.

Lanny said, "Sure, but for the moment let's assume that our killers have some connection with this affair. All right, where are the bodies?"

Scheer nodded. "There's no blood, no marks of violence. Could be the bank employees were forced out with the gunnies?"

Lanny said, "That's a possibility." He was looking at the massive door of the strong room. "What time does this branch close, Halladan?" The district manager looked up from a pile of high denomination bills and told him.

Lanny said, "Patrolman Kippax was shot less than fifteen minutes after that. Given a few minutes to collect the dough, then it would take most of the remaining time for 'em to get up to the river road."

Scheer said, "Meaning?"

"The sergeant at the roadblock didn't say anything about prisoners in the Pontiac."

"They might have been out of sight."

"Sure, though eight men take some fitting even into a big Pontiac."

Halladan said, "It would have to be nine. There's a janitor on the staff, and he'd be here with the manager and the clerks at that time,"

So Lanny said, "You couldn't hide four men inside a car containing five gunnies. And no prisoners or bodies were found in the abandoned Pontiac down by the pier head, and they'd had little time in which to dispose of prisoners on their way back in."

"So?" And now the G-men were looking at that big steel door.

Lanny strolled over to examine it. There was a dial on it, but it was set between two code letters. "So I think they're inside here, nicely tucked out of the way. And my guess is they shoved a few laggard customers inside, too."

Halladan said, "My God, then they're as good as dead, the lot of them,"

Lanny said, "Haven't you got keys for the safe?"

Halladan said, "You don't have keys for this type of safe. It's a time safe. You set this dial to a time and then shut the door, and then not even hell and high water can get it open until the time fixed."

"And then it opens automatically?"

Halladan said, "Yes," looking bleakly at the safe door. He went on, "It's really a safe; it's hardly big enough to be called a strong room. And if there are any people inside, they'll be dead by eight when it opens tomorrow."

He turned desperately. "You don't seem to understand. This damn' thing's fireproof, soundproof, and insulated against air. They'll be suffocated in a matter of hours!"

CHAPTER EIGHT
THE NET CLOSES

Haim Joannou—Pretty Boy—lifted his head and looked seaward in horror. That was his picture there, walking with the dame he'd picked up, and by it was an enlargement of his face. It had suffered in the printing, but still it came out unmistakably as...Pretty Boy.

"My God," whispered Joannou. "How the hell did they get that picture of me?"

When he'd picked up that girl he hadn't intended doing what he did, but he'd found himself knocking her about and getting more and more excited, and then suddenly that fury of emotion that was always simmering had boiled up—and over.

He hadn't intended to kill her, and when he found she wasn't struggling any more, wouldn't ever struggle again, he hadn't been concerned. She was a street trollop; anything could happen to that kind.

He had walked calmly away thinking: They don't know me here—few people do in New York. They'll never get on my track.

There'd been some anxiety at first, of course, imagining that people were turning and cops were looking hard at him. And he hadn't slept well that first night, mainly because he had decided not to go to the room he had rented since his arrival in the capital, and instead had dossed down in a very obscure and not very comfortable boarding house on Manhattan. So next day he had felt tired and grey, and the first head-lining of the case hadn't read nice to him and he hadn't in consequence bought a paper since.

He'd felt he hadn't needed to. He'd felt so safe. Especially in Freshwater.

And now he was reading that not only had they his photograph, linking him with the murdered girl, but they also knew he was in Freshwater. They gave the time of his arrival in a fudge column, and there was a description of the clothes he was wearing, emphasising the brightness of his classy check sports jacket.

There was also an item that said that the Vigilantes had been called out to help the police cordon off the town.

It was at that moment that Pretty Boy began to feel that Freshwater was a very tiny place indeed....

That infernal police car came cruising down the harbour road again. And this time, though he faced out to sea, Pretty Boy was listening, straining as though his life depended on it, as perhaps it did.

That booming voice with the ragged edges that always comes with a radio amplifier—"You are asked to cooperate with the police. A man, wanted for questioning in New York, is believed to be here in Freshwater. His picture and description are in a special edition now on sale in the town. You are asked to read this edition, then check up on every man you see. If citizens will cooperate we can get our man. Citizens of Freshwater, you are asked to cooperate...." All over again. One car cruising round the town and spinning a web from which it seemed impossible for him to escape.

Pretty Boy could think quickly, though. He moved swiftly down the beach steps and trudged through the sand towards the back of a line of beach chalets. He saw a red costume drying on a line, saw that this chalet was deserted for the moment.

He slipped inside, undressed in record time, and pulled on the damp swim trunks. Then he wrapped his clothes in a bundle and walked calmly back on to the beach. The cops were looking for a man in a bright sports jacket. A man in swim trunks didn't look quite the same.

Pretty Boy's next move was instinctive and characteristic.

He put his bundle down against the beach wall, where other bathers' clothes were. That separated him completely from the sports jacket that suddenly seemed too attractive. Then he walked along the beach until he saw a girl alone—and not a girl reading a newspaper, either.

He put on a good act. Went up, smiling, calling, "What ho, Thelma. Where've you been lately?" And with that, still talking, he sat beside her and knocked the sand off his calves and threw the wavy black hair out of his eyes.

And then turned and looked squarely at the girl.

And let his voice trail off; looked at the girl in horror. He was a good actor.

He said, "Well, for crying out loud, I thought you were a girl I knew." But he didn't make to get up. Instead he looked the more closely at her and said, "And you don't look a bit like her, now I see you close to. What'n heck's gone wrong with my eyes?"

She was laughing. He knew things were all right now. He'd make her do anything he wanted from now on. Though all he wanted at the moment was just to sit out prominently on that beach with her.

That seemed the safest place in Freshwater, that afternoon. They'd he looking for one man; they'd ignore a couple of spooning bathers down on the sands....

Pretty Boy watched the sun descending. After a time he had a thirst that was as dry as New Mexico, and a hunger to match, but he wasn't moving off this beach until his face was safe from inquisitive stares. He wanted darkness before he tried to get away from Freshwater, and he wanted this girl's company until that moment.

Once or twice the girl threw out hints, but he didn't take them. At such times, to keep her mind off food and drink, he put on a top-line demonstration of the art of lovemaking, and that quieted her. As always, his study of the technique: was paying off dividends....

He didn't want to have the girl with him after dusk, so he was glad when she said, "I must go home and change."

He said, "Sure, and then?"

She dropped her eyes and murmured, "Isn't that up to you?" She was only a kid, around twenty, but lightly built, blonded on top of (probably) mousey hair. Blue eyes, and quite a looker.

Pretty Boy got ardent and said, "It sure is." He was cutting out the European accent because the hotel clerk back in New York had commented on it. "Honey, you go get changed, then we'll meet some place and have dinner together. Yeah?"

Her eyes gave the answer. Delighted! Pretty Boy could always depend on that sort of reception to his proposals.

He said, "Where and when?" There was that damned cop car swinging its headlights round the harbour, the speaker still going, instructing Freshwater citizens to cooperate in the detection of Pretty Boy.

The girl rose, a slim silhouette against the fading red of the western horizon.

"The clock tower, by Tissdan's," she said. "At nine."

He didn't know where the clock tower was, didn't intend to be there, anyway. But he said, yes, he'd be there, because that got rid of the dame.

They parted atop the beach steps. He had to play the gallant to the last. He said, "I must go get my clothes," then quickly took her in his arms and gave her a parting kiss. She said something about being recognised, her voice shaky, but she was pleased and she skipped happily away to catch a suburban bus.

Pretty boy turned—and forgot about the girl in an instant. That was Pretty Boy, always had been—use 'em and then forget 'em. And the girl had been useful.

He found his clothes and changed in the darkness by the overhanging beach wall. He took the contents out of the pockets of his betraying, colourful sports jacket and then buried it deeply in the sand above the tide-mark. It wasn't a cool evening and he'd be less conspicuous in his shirt than in that jacket.

He wanted a drink now, but for a time he kept away from the cafés because they looked too well lighted.

He passed the steamer booking office. It was closed. The next boat out was the following morning, a placard said. That was one avenue of escape that was barred to him. He walked briskly along the harbour wall towards the station hill. There were plenty of boats below, but he guessed it would be risky trying to untie one and negotiate the crowded harbour.

When he came to the station, he went in cautiously, keeping well back from the platform approach that was flooded with light,

There was a man in the uniform of the railroad police right by the barrier. He was leaning against it as though tired, but as a departing passenger hurried up he straightened quickly and scrutinised the man very hard....

Pretty Boy turned and walked out of the station yard. That was another door closed against him. He came back to the sea wall around the harbour and stood and watched the distant flashing of a light. He wondered what to do next.

There was no escape by sea or rail, and the last he'd heard there were Vigilantes in a tight cordon around the little town.

He ducked his head as twin headlights flashed along the protecting rail atop the wall. It was that cop car coming on another circuit. And the speaker was going again.

Only this time it was talking directly to him.

CHAPTER NINE
WHERE'S BONNIE?

The F.B.I. stepped forward to take control. "First things first," said Scheer brusquely. "We've gotta get these fellows out without delay—if they are inside. Get experts with blowlamps."

Lanny was already dialling. "We'll bring the Navy in. Their fellows are tops at cutting metal."

Halladan got excited and almost shouted, "You're wasting your time. We had a door stuck once and it took a couple of days to burn it open. It'll open itself long before you get through. Those chaps inside'll be lucky if they're alive right now."

Lanny got through to the Navy. When he replaced the receiver he said, "If you've got any better ideas, let's have 'em." Halladan hadn't. So Lanny said, "Okay, we do what we can with burners."

Scheer came across saying, "By God, there'll be no mercy for those gunnies if this raid's been the death of some fellows in there."

Lanny sat back, said carefully, "You've got to catch them first, G-man."

The way he said it brought Scheer round, eyes

narrowed. "They're here in Freshwater, aren't they?" Lanny shrugged. Scheer said, "Look, when we got the report we were told that the gunnies were trapped inside Freshwater. You've got cops and Vigilantes around the town, haven't you?"

Lanny sighed and rose slowly. "Make it past tense and I'm with you, brother," he said. Then he snapped, "I had them trapped. And we did have a useful army of Vigilantes covering every track and pathway out of the town, while my men watched the roads. But someone decided that Vigilantes weren't necessary and pulled 'em all in. For the last half hour the way's been wide open for anyone to walk out the back way," he ended bitterly.

The G-man thundered. "For Christ sake, who did that fool thing?" His companions came away from their clue-hunting to hear Lanny's answer.

Lanny said, "Ask the chief; he's coming in now."

A car had stopped outside. Murdoch was first in, bristling and aggressive; then the chief, older, heavier, and slower, shoved his scrubby brows round the corner and walked in after them. The desk-sergeant hadn't taken long to get through to the chief—and the chief hadn't taken long to get out to Green Hollow, either.

The chief said, "F.B.I.?" Scheer came out with his leather-cased card. The chief glared at Lanny, but his eyes were uneasy. He was wondering what in hell had been said against him to these dangerous F.B.I. operators. He must have decided that attack was the best method of defence for he rapped: "I thought I pulled you in off the job, Just?

Scheer and the other G-men looked quickly round at Lanny who said, calmly, "You did. But if you remember, I didn't say I'd do as you ordered. If you have any doubts on that score, I brought along a record of our conversation." He took it from his pocket.

The chief glared. And then he said, defensively, "The hell, if you think there's anything on that record to incriminate me in any way, you're mistaken."

"Yeah, I know," Lanny nodded. "That's why you were so careful in what you said at that meeting—you knew it was going on record. Well, there's nothing in it to incriminate me, either, so far as I remember." Suddenly he tossed the spool across to Scheer. "You hold on to that, buddy, and ask the chief why he pulled out the Vigilantes just when they were needed. If you don't like the answer, maybe you'll decide to hang on to that record until you can run it through."

Scheer said carefully, "Maybe you'll tell me why you decided to do without the Vigilantes, chief."

The chief kept up his glare. "Why the hell should I justify my actions to you?" he rapped. The chief was on a wheel and he couldn't get off, so he had to make the best of things. Again he attacked, "The F.B.I. have no authority over a local police force. Where a Federal offence is committed you have to be called in, and we are expected to cooperate as fully as possible with you. But that doesn't put you over me," he thundered.

It could have been light rain falling on a duck's back, the effect it had on a hardened campaigner like Scheer.

He said, "We know all that, chief, and you don't need to answer me. But I ask again, why did you call in the Vigilantes?"

The chief chuntered inside his thick throat for a moment and then said, defiantly, "I'm not having any armed mobs chasing around my town, regardless of the titles they give themselves. There's people in Freshwater to say they're not satisfied that this Vigilance Committee's on the up and up."

Scheer interrupted. "Why was Captain Just suspended in the middle of a double murder hunt?" His strong, bronzed face gave no sign of the thought behind the question.

The chief barked, "When I give orders, I expect 'em to be obeyed. And I ordered Just to take the Vigilantes off the hunt and he did nothing of the sort, so I suspended him. So now what are you going to do about it?"

Scheer didn't hesitate. He was a fast thinker—and a good judge of men. He said, "Taking the Vigilantes out of the cordon leaves holes—big holes. It gives six men, wanted on murder charges, a chance to thumb their noses at us and get away. What are you going to do about it?"

The chief said, "I've pulled every available man out of the town to watch the back roads."

Scheer said, "It can't be enough. Now, what objection have you to pulling the Vigilantes back for just this one operation? They're vitally necessary."

The chief licked his lips. Lanny felt almost sorry for the old chiseller.

He had a story, and now he was stuck with it! He had to come back with the same story.

"They're a lot of armed hoodlums, and citizens have complained about them. Crime's no place for amateur cops. We'll get by without them."

Scheer looked at his fellow G-men. He said, "We can't do a thing about it—if that's your decision, chief, that's what it's got to be. But you take responsibility for your actions, you know." he suddenly rapped back.

The chief swallowed as though something had hurt him. Then he cracked, "You don't have to remind me."

He swung on Lanny, the cause of this jarring meeting with the F.B.I. He said, roughly, "Captain, you were suspended an hour ago. It still stands. So far as Freshwater's concerned. You're just another civilian." He was in a savage temper.

Lanny looked at Scheer. He knew that Scheer wasn't impressed by the chief's bluster. Very carefully Lanny said, "I'm just a civilian—you heard that, didn't you? But I reckon I'm a very useful citizen right now because I know more about crime and Freshwater than most men. Okay, I'm volunteering my services to the F.B.I.—if they'll have 'em."

The chief took fright and roared, "What the hell, no busted cop of mine's going to play at G-man in Freshwater!"

Scheer had had enough. He came slowly over to the chief. "Look," he said, "we don't want trouble. We want to catch these gunnies, that's all. And you want my opinion? It's a queer cop that'd pull out a bunch of

Vigilantes in an emergency like this—unless he was made to do so."

The chief went white, the way the G-man spoke to him. And there was more to come.

"Over in Mason County we've heard stories about a big-time racketeer who's supposed to have a police chief sewn up. It wouldn't be you, would it?" The chief lifted his head, and there was fear in his eyes. His world, built of a compound of greed and indolence, had begun to tumble down in this last half-hour or so.

Scheer said, still very quietly, "I don't see how we can do without the services of a man as valuable as Captain Just. If you insist on his suspension I'm going to enlist him, because of his special knowledge, to assist the F.B.I. So, what's it got to be, chief?"

The chief suddenly found his voice, exploded, "Do what the hell you like," and went stumbling back to his car.

Scheer turned to the big police captain. There was a little smile on his face. "Maybe we'd better consider you're still in the force, eh, captain?"

Lanny wasn't in humorous mood. He was looking after the chief. He said, "That's a desperate man, Scheer, and it's the presence of you G-men here that's got him nervy. You know where he's going now?"

Scheer said, "To talk to his boss—Racketeer Myrtle."

Lanny showed his surprise. "You guys know a lot."

They walked over to the door together. There was the usual crowd on the sidewalk, and not a cop anywhere to keep them under control. A Navy truck came whipping up the hill at speed just then.

Scheer said, "We've been learning, lately. But not enough to move in on yet. The F.B.I. can't operate anywhere anytime; there must be some Federal offence or else a call for help from the local police chief." He watched the confident young naval officer as he came pushing through the crowd. "It was nice of the chief to forget this record," he smiled, playing with the spool in his hand.

Lanny said, "There's nothing on it that openly indicts anyone."

Then the Navy were in, apparatus and all. The smart young officer nodded to Lanny, was swiftly introduced to the F.B.I., then crossed to the massive safe door. Lanny said, "Well?"

The officer turned. "Come back some time tomorrow and we might have something to show for our work."

Lanny said, "You'll only find corpses inside, then, if it takes so long." So he said, "Look, concentrate on making an air hole. If we can get a tube inside we can keep 'em alive until the damn' thing opens itself."

Halladan came round bleating. "What the hell, they must be dead now. And Czanik, he was a good guy. I don't like to think of it."

Lanny crossed to the door. Scheer was looking out at the gawkers, scowling as if he didn't care for them.

Back of the crowd a car started up and then eased off on a road that came out by the harbour. At the wheel was a man with the elegance of a doughnut—a bald little man, with sharp eyes set in a heavy face that was curiously flat-cheeked.

A little man who was jumpy with excitement because for the first time in his life be had chance to get his dirty-nailed hands on ten grand...ten thousand of Uncle Sam's greenbacks.

Marty Dimenza was on his way back with his car, ready to take the New York mobsters out when darkness fell. Both Lanny and the G-man saw him, saw his car—and saw dozens of other car-owners crowding up for a near view of the drama, the race to save the lives of some imprisoned, slowly suffocating men. So they thought nothing of it.

The G-man spoke jerkily out of the corner of his mouth. "We can't do any good here, captain. It's out of our hands now. I'm going down with my men to look the gunnies' Pontiac over."

Lanny hesitated. He didn't know what to do. These G-men were competent, and now the bank robbery and killing of Patrolman Kippax were their meat. His, he knew, was the tracking of Pretty Boy. Better leave them to their job and concentrate on his own, he thought. But how to start again?

Until the chief, through pressure on him, had interfered, he had been developing a sound plan to pull in the killer. Now, with the Vigilantes in their homes and nearly all the cops withdrawn from the town area to provide a sketchy cordon, he didn't know where to begin.

So he said, "I'll come with you." He might just as well.

There was a patrolman guarding the gunnies' car. He looked gingerly at Lanny; evidently he had heard of the trouble with the chief, and probably didn't know that Lanny was back on the job.

Lanny said, briskly, "Anybody touched this car?"

The patrolman said, "Only Lieutenant Murdoch earlier, and the fingerprint boys."

So the G-men set in work on their own account, photographing and fingerprinting and then getting the Pontiac towed away to the police HQ.

While they were still working. Lieutenant Murdoch came roaring up on the motorcycle that he generally effected. Lanny suddenly got an idea that Murdoch was wanting to get friendly; maybe the sight of G-men in the town had shaken him up a little. He was a bit of a rat, anyway.

He stood astraddle the machine and shoved back his goggles. "I thought you might like to know," he began. "There's an epidemic of lost people in Freshwater. In the last half-hour we've had another five people enquiring about missing husbands. They are all people who use that bust-up bank."

"Five?" That jolted Lanny. He went back to the G-men. "Looks like there are around ten people in that safe back in Green Hollow," he told them.

Scheer came up from the back floorboards. He was tough, but the import of the news shook him. He said, softly, "They've got little chance, then. Those mobsters couldn't have known what they were doing, or they wouldn't have condemned so many to death. But that's no excuse—they did it, and now we've got to find them."

Lanny turned away. "Sure, sure. And I'll leave you to it. I'm going to pick up my own jalopy and see what's being done about Pretty Boy."

Half an hour later he was back on the hunt in his own car, shoving new ideas into the search. It seemed he was again in authority, for no one disobeyed when he gave an order. And the chief was keeping so well out of everybody's way that he hadn't been seen since his trek out to Green Hollow earlier.

Sergeant Pedersen was touring the town, talking to the population and urging them to cooperate in the search for the woman-slayer. Not that they needed any persuading. That day the local newspaper had record sales. Probably every literate person in the town went around carrying a copy, and there were no half-measures about it—people *did* look at every man they met, *did* check to see if he answered the description. It got so that you weren't safe wearing a sports jacket at all.

Lanny saw Pedersen and pulled his jalopy in ahead to stop him. He got out and spoke to the big blond sergeant.

Pedersen's throat was going sore through doing so much talking. "You'd have thought we'd have found the rat by now," he complained. "Jeez, if he's here at all he's found a hole for certain. It ain't possible for a guy to be unidentified in Freshwater this long, otherwise."

Lanny said. "That's the trouble. He can't be on the

streets. He must be hiding away some place." Wherein he was wrong.

He looked savagely along the harbour road, with its hotels and blocks of bright, modern apartments and attractive shops and restaurants, and the jumble of masts and funnels in the harbour opposite.

"God blast the chief for what he's done," he exploded. "If he'd left me with those good guys, the Vigilantes, I'd have had picked men go through every hotel and apartment block in town. I'd have driven the rat out of his hole. I'd have found him."

"Sure, I know how you feel." A big sedan stopped just behind the patrol car, but neither noticed it. Pedersen went in. "Ain't there no way of getting the Vigilantes back to help?"

"Boss Myrtle's said no, so the chief's got to say no. And he's still the chief," said Lanny bitterly. The sidewalk seemed suddenly to have grown very congested. "You'd better get some grease for your throat and try and talk that lug into the open," he said. "I've got a plan, and I think it'll work—but I've got to have fifty men relieved from watching roads first."

Pedersen's eyes were fixed over his shoulder. Lanny was saying, "By God, I've got to get the chief to change his mind," when someone touched his shoulder lightly.

He turned. Boss Myrtle was right back of him, heavy and glowering, and flanking him were his apes. They had that tense, curiously rigid stance of men about to go into sudden and violent action.

Boss Myrtle's voice gravelled up, "Where's Bonnie?

What've you done with her?"

CHAPTER TEN
VIGILANTES RETURN

Lanny felt the blood drain slowly from his face. And it wasn't fear that did it, not fear for himself.

"Bonnie?" he said quickly. "What's the matter with Bonnie?" His heart began to bump. He'd been dodging Bonnie Myrtle, the boss's daughter, for weeks, because she *was* the boss's daughter. But that wasn't because he was allergic to her—if there was one girl he'd ever met who should be Mrs. Lanny Just, it was happy, laughing...and innocent Bonnie.

Bonnie, who didn't know that the wealth that made life a dream for her was crooked money. That her father was a hard and ruthless racketeer who ran the police of Freshwater, took 'protection' money from legitimate businesses, and operated a number of quite illegal businesses himself.

Bonnie didn't know that, and Lanny Just wasn't the man to be able to tell her. How can you tell the nicest girl you know that her father is a bigshot crook, and you're out to bust him and shove him for life into a pen?

There seemed no future for Bonnie in Lanny's life,

but this didn't prevent his heart from kicking over at the thought of harm having come to her.

Boss Myrtle's eyes were narrowed pinpoints of ferocity. He hated this big, athletic police captain, had hated him ever since the name of Bonnie had fallen from his lips. He was a hard and brutally callous man in everything except where it related to his daughter. But where Bonnie was concerned, he revealed a completely unsuspected side to his character.

He doted on her; he was so proud of her, lavished everything on the girl—clothes, presents, holidays, even a car. She had all the affection of which he was capable, and for that reason there was none left over for anyone else.

It had given him a shock, to hear a police captain speaking of affection between him, Lanny, and his daughter—the shock that all fathers get when suddenly they realise that their child is growing away from them. And an enemy, a cop, at that. Now Boss Myrtle was savagely jealous, in a fury against the cause of his emotional disturbance.

And he was alarmed, too, alarmed about the absent girl.

He snarled, "I'm asking you, Just—where's Bonnie? And don't give back any hand-off answers or you'll regret it."

Lanny eased from the police car, his muscles bunching. Ice crackled in his voice when he spoke. "Myrtle, goddam you, if you threaten me I'll stick you in jug, just see if I don't! Sergeant, get out of that car; I might need you. The hell, you won't shove me around, not with twice as many apes as you've got with you!"

Boss Myrtle looked into those biting eyes and knew that this time he had met his match. This was one man who was not to be moved by threats any more than bribes hadn't touched him. And he knew that if he came out with another insult, the police captain would try to keep his word—and jail him! He saw Lanny's hand on the butt of his gun holster and knew that the fellow wouldn't hesitate to use it on him; back of his mind he remembered Lanny talking about wooden suits—and hoping there was one that would fit him, Boss Myrtle.

He growled, "Keep your skin on. I'm asking you, where's Bonnie?"

"I'm telling you," rapped Lanny, "I don't know. I saw her some days ago—and I didn't want to see her then. She's phoned me a few times since, but I've kept saying no. For me and Bonnie there ain't no future with you around. Boss, blast you! Why the hell had you to get yourself such a fine daughter?"—bitterly.

Boss Myrtle didn't understand all that Lanny was saying, but he did get one thing and believed it—that Lanny didn't know where his daughter was.

It disturbed him even more. His concern for the girl was so great that he began to show weakness before his enemy. Heavy lips parted as his tongue licked away a sudden dryness. He said, hoarsely, "You can't think where she might be?" And now his eyes were grey with misery.

Lanny understood.

"Pretty Boy? You're scared something might happen to her while that maniac's in town?" Myrtle didn't say anything. Lanny found his pulse beginning to race as he thought of it himself. Back in the chief's office he remembered talking about Pretty Boy and the possibility of the murderer hurting someone else—perhaps Bonnie. He hadn't really meant it himself; had been talking rather wildly, angrily, at the time. But perhaps he had sown an idea in Boss Myrtle's mind, and it had grown and was now beginning to flower.

He shrugged away his own momentary spasm of disquietude. An idea was beginning to mount in his brain; maybe he could turn this paternal streak to advantage. It was a long shot, but it was worth trying, though he hated having to do it.

He said, to give himself time to think, "You've searched the town thoroughly?"

Boss Myrtle nodded. "I've had a couple of dozen men going from end to end. I'm just going to get a street talkie car on the prowl. But—God, where can she have hidden herself?"

It startled and disturbed Lanny, too. Freshwater was only a small place. He knew Bonnie's tastes and habits pretty well by now, and he couldn't imagine where she had put herself. He pulled himself together; of course there was no danger to her from Pretty Boy, and he mustn't get to thinking there was. Murderers don't often repeat their crimes, not unless they are crazy.

Boss Myrtle seemed to be following his thoughts. "This Pretty Boy guy," he grated. "He seems screwball enough for anything. I want Bonnie out of town until he's captured."

So Lanny said, "You and a lot of other people, Boss. You're not the only one. By now half the women in Freshwater are hysterical, I'll bet, crazy with fear for themselves or their children. And if you hadn't interfered with my plans, maybe by now he'd be safe under lock and key."

Boss Myrtle ground out, "I don't give a damn about other people."

"You don't have to tell me that." Lanny was cynical. He turned to go back to his car. "But you're mighty concerned now that Bonnie's disappeared, aren't you? Well, okay, since you're temporary head of the Freshwater police, give the order for the Vigilantes to go out and watch the roads, so that I can put my men to combing the town. It's about the last time you'll be able to tell the police what to do, anyway!"

He was walking away. Boss Myrtle rapped, "What do you mean by that crack, Just?"

Lanny turned coolly. "Your reign's near to an end, Boss. I'm not telling you anything the chief won't tell you when you next meet. But here's news for you. The F.B.I. are in town, and they already know quite a bit about a two-timing police chief who does as a no-good racketeer tells him."

If he had hoped to see a change on Boss Myrtle's heavy countenance, he was disappointed. Boss just nodded, as though his mind was on other things, as indeed it was.

Lanny went his rounds and then drove out to Green Hollow. A couple of cops had been brought in to keep the road clear, but there was a big crowd all along the street, heads turned towards the bank, passing from mouth to mouth any item of news that came out concerning the race to save the lives of the trapped men.

Lanny stood in the main bank room and watched the Navy men at work with their burners. They had been a couple of hours on the job already, and Lanny's heart sank as he saw the smallness of the results. Hope for the suffocating men inside was very small, if this was as fast as they could get a hole in through the door to them.

He saw one of the F.B.I. men pushing his way through the crowd and went across to speak to him. Dusk was coming, and the light gave an unreal effect to the drama.

The G-man said, "We got plenty of prints. We've already traced the car—it was stolen a couple of weeks ago out at Rochester. But we've got no lead on where the gunnies are. My guess is they've got friends here in Freshwater and they're lying doggo."

Lanny said, "That's what Pretty Boy's doing. He's hiding some place off the streets for certain."

Wherein Lanny was wrong, of course. It hadn't occurred to him or to anyone else in Freshwater that the safest place to hide was right where everyone could see you, out on the wide, sunny sands.

Lanny was restless. He had to keep moving. Back of

his mind was a growing unease: he couldn't keep his thoughts off Bonnie.

He prowled around, for some reason mostly keeping to the coast roads and around the harbour. He was tooling along by the Fun Park, now sparkling with flashing coloured lights, when he heard a loudspeaker booming, "Calling Bonnie Myrtle, calling Bonnie Myrtle. Bonnie Myrtle is urgently wanted at her home. Will all persons who have seen her since noon today please phone Freshwater 2554."

Lanny pulled up by the kerb, his blood running suddenly cold. That meant that so far all the searching for Bonnie hadn't found her. This time he couldn't stop himself from connecting her disappearance with the presence of Pretty Boy in Freshwater.

Pretty Boy, who had torn one woman to pieces in his lust already....

He stabbed for the starter, almost in a panic as thoughts crowded into his brain. He saw Bonnie walking somewhere in Freshwater. Saw someone joining her. Him. Pretty Boy. Such a soft, pleasant talker, that woman receptionist had said at the New York hotel. Perhaps he had talked softly, persuasively to Bonnie. And Bonnie was such a kid; she could have gone off with him just for the hell of it. Not meaning badly, of course; she wasn't that kind.

But if she had gone with that killer....

Captain Lanny Just broke a few police regulations himself in the next few minutes.

Boss Myrtle lived out in the suburbs, but Lanny

knew that the Freshwater phone number was that of his 'business' address. Boss used a betting station, housed in a big seafront block, for his headquarters. It was ablaze with light as he pulled up outside.

He went straight up to Myrtle's floor. As he pushed open the swing doors he thought, "I'm sticking my head right between the lion's teeth." If Boss Myrtle wanted to go through with his unspoken desire to rub him out, he, Lanny, was presenting him with a first-class opportunity.

But Lanny had guts, as must people in Freshwater knew, and the situation was desperate enough to demand the boldest measures.

A couple of apes in the outer office came up to their feet as he pushed through. Their dirty little eyes were incredulous. Then a door opened and Alastair Myrtle began to come out of a smaller office. He started when he saw Lanny, and then that easy smile came to his handsome, Army-officer type face. And Lanny liked that smile a lot less than the shifty unease of the apes.

Lanny rapped, "Where's Boss Myrtle?"

Alastair inclined his head sideways, his smiling eyes covering a brain that was thinking rapidly.

Lanny quoted, "'Walk into my parlour, said the spider to the fly'. Okay. I'll walk in—spider!"

Alastair stood aside, his smile even larger. As Lanny strode past Alastair said, "Go on, big mouth, hand me out the big wisecracks. You and Bob Hope should get together—if you live long enough."

Lanny came into the big, sleek, expensively

appointed office. Boss Myrtle saw him enter, and hope leaped into his face. It died as Lanny grimly shook his head.

"No, Boss, I don't know where Bonnie is. You haven't heard anything?"

Boss Myrtle sank back, his face showing the torment of his mind. "Not a thing. She's never done this before, been away so long without telling me where she was going. Something's happened to her."

They were enemies, these men facing each other across the desk, but their love for Bonnie united them at this moment. Now they had thought for nothing except the safety of the girl.

Lanny said, "She might he out of town, of course."

"Without telling me she was going?" Myrtle's face was haggard. "She hasn't got the use of her car; it's been under repair for nearly a week now."

And Lanny knew that, too. He said, slowly, "I'm thinking she must be out of town. Someone must have given her a lift. I only hope—" He stopped.

"Well?"

"I only hope the driver wasn't Pretty Boy, that's all."

He could see the way Boss Myrtle shook that the racketeer's nerves were in a bad way. He thought it was curious—Boss Myrtle had turned the heat on many a man in his life, had beaten up his opponents and enemies without the slightest compunction. Yet now, because a chit of a girl couldn't be found for a few hours, he was worrying himself blue with anxiety.

Lanny knew that this was the time to press home

with his plans. He said, "If you hadn't stepped in, Boss, I'd have had Pretty Boy in jail by now. Then you wouldn't be suffering."

Alastair came quietly into the room at that moment. Lanny looked at him contemptuously. He knew that the younger Myrtle had been outside to make sure that Lanny's presence within the crooks' HQ wasn't some sort of a police trap. Even now Alastair wasn't sure, couldn't believe that the police captain had walked in without apparent protection.

Lanny turned to Boss Myrtle. "Maybe it isn't too late to do something about Pretty Boy now, Boss." Boss Myrtle's eyes came up to meet his, but they didn't register any emotion. Lanny leaned forward, his jaw muscles tightening because this was to be a kind of showdown. "I hate like hell to have to come to you, a crooked wire-puller, to get police work done, Boss, but I'm doing it.

"I want to get the Vigilantes out. I want to go into every house, hotel, and apartment in Freshwater and check on the people there. I want to recruit several hundred Vigilantes—aye, a thousand if they'll volunteer, and I think they will. If Pretty Boy's in Freshwater, I intend to find him. If Bonnie's in Freshwater, we'll find her, too. I only hope to God we find her unharmed!"

Boss Myrtle sat with his big hands clasped on the broad polished desk before him. After a time his voice rasped, "What do you want me to do?"

Lanny told him. "Get through to the chief. The chief won't ask for the help of the Vigilantes because he's already said they're a rabble of no-goods and trouble-makers—he was following the line you'd set up. Okay, he's got to be made to give way, and you're the one person who can do it. Do what you've been doing for a long time, Boss," he said cynically. "Tell the chief what to do."

Myrtle grated, "You're asking me to commit suicide." He was looking beyond Lanny at his brother.

And Alastair was alarmed and for once wasn't smiling. He came into the conversation, his voice quick with anger. "Don't let him kid you, Boss. It's all a trick to get the Vigilantes in strong. Give 'em this opportunity and how long do you think we'll last in Freshwater? They'll come gunning for us first thing!"

Boss Myrtle let his eyes trail back to Lanny. Lanny said, brutally, "So what? It's only a question of time, Boss, before you get yours. The F.B.I. have got a smell of what's happening here in Freshwater, and when they start to move in on a job, they do it pretty thoroughly, don't they? You and Brother Alastair will be wearing pretty clothes soon—Federal issue!"

For the first time in his life Lanny, heard Boss Myrtle indulge in humour. "I thought you wanted to see me in a wooden suit, captain?"

Lanny rose. "That'd please me. Boss. I want Bonnie, but that can never be while you're dirtying up the burg."

Boss said, "You're one helluva son-in-law, Just," but there was a light in his eyes. Maybe he was seeing the inevitable; maybe he was realising that when the end came for him it would be better for his beloved daughter to have the protection of some straight guy... someone like this tough-talking. courageous young police captain.

His hand reached out towards the phone. Alastair came across snarling and grabbed it. Lanny realised that the office door had been left slightly open. saw a dirty mean eye slitted there in the gap.

He found himself punching, hitting with all the strength of his big-muscled shoulders. Alastair keeled over, crashed on to a chair that broke under his sudden weight, and when he got up, his face was white with pain and he was holding his thigh where he had bruised himself.

He found himself looking into the muzzle of Lanny's Colt.

"Quit stroking yourself and put your hands over your head," ordered Lanny. He kicked the door open and covered the apes in the outer office. Some more hoods came out of a smoke-filled room across, hearing the noise. Lanny covered the lot. He said to Boss Myrtle, "Now get on the phone."

Boss sat tight in his chair. Suddenly he was the old Boss again, resolute and threatening. "What the hell," he roared. "Who's boss round here?" He was glaring at his brother. "If I want to ring the police chief, I'm gonna ring him, see?"

He turned on Lanny. "Put that gun away; you don't need it while I'm boss. And you—" to his apes—"get to hell away from that door. Start packing—*the F.B.I. are on to us and we're pulling out*!"

When he heard that, Lanny put away his gun. He knew things were going to be all right. He started to walk towards the door. Behind him he heard Boss Myrtle dialling. He didn't wait to hear what was said to the police chief; he knew that when Boss Myrtle gave an order, it had to be obeyed.

He drove furiously back to HQ and started giving orders on his own account. Radio messages flashed out to all units. Within ten minutes the town was in a turmoil of excitement.

The big drive to find Pretty Boy had begun.

Only by now Lanny was thinking of it as a drive to find Bonnie Myrtle, too.

CHAPTER ELEVEN
PRETTY BOY
GETS AN IDEA

It wasn't quite dark when a battered sedan pulled out of a narrow street down among the warehouses. The driver was a shapeless man, bald under his velour, with long sagging cheeks that touched his upturned collar. He was a small-time crook with ten grand to intoxicate his brain. He bungled the gear change on the hill out from the harbour area; he was nervous.

Alongside him five men huddled, silent, their eyes watching quickly from side to side. Only one stirred. He shoved his scraggy neck like a tortoise's up from his collar, and his vague wandering eyes caught street lights and reflected them and he looked zanier than ever. That sloppy grin came to bare his broken teeth as, after a while, he whispered, "Ain't we gonna have no gun-play? I was promised. And we ain't done no shootin', not for a long time. I guess I like shootin'."

Eddy Eitel looked at him with repulsion and said, "There ain't gonna be no shootin', not if Dim's on the level."

There was menace...threat...in his tone. Dim stirred

uneasily at the wheel. To change the subject he said, "There's a cop car goin' by. What's it sayin' now?" They listened. They seemed to hear one word—it could have been "Vigilantes," but at that they might have been mistaken.

Gino suddenly spoke, "The hell with cop cars! We ain't stoppin' to listen to that. All afternoon it's been goin'. That and the talkie car askin' Bonnie Myrtle to go home to daddy. Who the hell's Bonnie Myrtle, anyway?"

Marty Dimenza said, "Oh, some big shot's daughter, I guess," offhandedly. Then they were away from the harbour and turning along the highway that led west.

They would have saved themselves time and trouble if they had stopped to listen to that police car....

Pretty Boy froze on the railing as the amplified voice boomed across to him. It was Sergeant Pedersen and he was saying, "Calling Pretty Boy, calling Pretty Boy. You will save yourself a lot of trouble if you will go to the nearest police officer and give yourself up."

There was satisfaction in the sergeant's voice as he went crooning on, "Pretty Boy, Pretty Boy, you haven't a chance now. The Vigilantes are out almost shoulder to shoulder round Freshwater. We're watching the airport, the rail station, the harbour entrance."

Pretty Boy's eyes saw for the first time the significance of an idling motor-craft across the narrow entrance to the harbour. A searchlight suddenly streamed from it and lit up the array of vessels quietly dipping to the gentle Atlantic swell that crept in round the breakwaters.

"Pretty Boy, Pretty Boy, you're in a hopeless position. Give yourself up right now. All over town citizens are being enlisted as Vigilantes. In one hour we're going to start a house-to-house search. So, Pretty Boy, why not save us all this trouble? If you are innocent of that New York crime, you will have opportunity to save yourself before a United States court of justice. If you do not give yourself up—" Petersen's voice was suddenly harsh with menace—"you run the risk of being lynched by Freshwater citizens!

"Pretty Boy, they're after you now! *Your best chance is to give yourself up!*"

It was Pedersen's voice, but it was really Lanny speaking. Lanny wanted to force Pretty Boy into surrendering. It would save a lot of trouble if he did— and that was no idle warning of lynching. If Pretty Boy got into the wrong hands, he'd have no opportunity of ever defending himself in a court of justice.

Pretty Boy knew it, too. There were people passing; he heard snatches of conversation, and it was all about him. As the minutes passed he could feel the temper of the crowd growing rougher, more ill-disposed towards him. The town had had enough of Pretty Boy for one day.

Pretty Boy began to feel conspicuous, standing there alone against the rail. He decided he would be safer moving along with the crowd. So long as he kept his face averted when he came to lights he should be safe.

But walking with the crowd wasn't reassuring. It

consisted mostly of men. patrolling the streets with the idea of being around if Pretty Boy was discovered. Their womenfolk were mostly indoors.

Pretty Boy got the reek of liquor in his face and a little fellow started yammering up at him. "We oughta do to the buzzard what he did to that girl. We oughta rip his guts out, I tell ya. Me, I'm gonna do it if I lay hands on him."

Someone in front turned. "Yeah, that's what I say. What the hell, all this trouble just to try a guy. We could save the state a lot of money, I reckon."

They were all talking, all around him. All men, all saying the same thing. Pretty Boy walked in their midst and kept his mouth shut. He wasn't going to invite attention to himself with that European accent maybe betraying him.

He walked, he listened, and his mind was curiously cool and detached now. He was in a trap and he knew it, and it was not his way to get panicky at a time when he had the most need of his powers of reasoning.

He told himself. "This is hopeless. I've no place to go, nowhere to hide my face for long. Once they get down to it, I'm going to be identified. I've been lucky so far—it can't last much longer."

So he set to work coolly to use his brain, to think of the best way out of this situation.

And obviously the best way was not to be caught by this savage, blood-lusting mob.

He listened again.

"We oughta get him and pull him apart between

two cars." It was his friend, the little alcoholic. He had imagination, and the drink was hotting it up. And the crowd wanted to listen to talk like that.

Pretty Boy told himself dispassionately: Yeah? If I'm going to be caught, better let a cop catch me!

Not that that gave him much chance of survival. In the end they'd rip his trousers and fix moist pads on to his legs and arms, and there'd be a metal skull-cap over his close-shaved head. They said that an electro-cuted man didn't suffer—much. But Pretty Boy, who had caused so much suffering in his time, didn't want to suffer at all. He hated physical pain and would do anything rather than submit to it.

All this talk about having a chance to prove himself innocent before a court of justice was bunk—he told himself. He wasn't innocent. He had killed the girl in the way the papers hinted. And he knew that once found he hadn't a chance—not with that damning photograph, and then the evidence of the hotel people who had seen him with the girl within minutes of her death.

If the cops got him, he'd take a last walk from a cell in Death Row that would end in a room with one chair in it....

They were getting worked up, this crowd, inflaming each other with their primitive passions.

"The hell," someone was saying. "Don't even let me see a cop with the guy. That sonofabitch ain't fit to live, and he ain't gonna live, not if I c'n do anything about it!"

Then someone else jeered, "You talk! You know what'll happen? That guy'll get picked up by the cops, and they'll stand him before a judge, and a crooked lawyer will plead 'guilty but insane,' and then they'll put him in a bughouse till everyone's forgotten about the affair."

"Sure, sure," another voice came floating back through the darkness. "Don't it always happen? These guys that can afford hotels and fancy women, they can buy themselves outa anything. Guess Pretty Boy'll turn out to be someone big—so big they won't want to touch him. Justice is like the Freshwater police—rotten. So help me, they won't need justice for this guy if I'm around!"

Even then, while men were growling savage approval all around him, the idea didn't come to Pretty Boy. He was still trying to figure a way out of the jam, not quite listening to what was being said.

For one thing, he was now so thirsty he didn't think he could last out much longer without a drink. He was hungry, too, but he didn't notice the pangs because of that raging, fiery torment in his mouth and throat. That long wait on the hot beach hadn't been altogether pleasure....

He came to an abrupt halt, his eyes on a machine. It was an automat, fixed round the walls of a self-serve cafeteria. Pretty Boy stood back, letting the crowd drift by, figuring out how to get at the coke bottles inside the automat.

If he could get inside without being detected, he

stood a good chance. He could sit facing the wall, at one of the high stools all around the room; could put his nickel in, and get as much coke and as many wrapped packets of eats as he wanted. And he wanted a lot. Wanted it so much, he took the risk.

And won out.

No one shouted, no one cried out an alarm as he went quickly in and got up on a seat. Now he fell safe, looking into this corner. Just back of him were a couple; they helped to screen him.

He slid his money in and grabbed the coke as though life were contained in it. Pulled the cap off under the shelf and drank it straight off. It was miraculous, how good he felt when that was done.

When he had drained it, he even sat for a minute to enjoy the feeling of refreshment that came with the cool coke. They were talking, some people across the room. Loudly. About him, of course.

He got another coke and pulled the cap off and started to drink. Back of him the couple were whispering, yet curiously he heard their whispers above the noise of street traffic outside, above the chatter in the cafeteria.

The man sounded peevish. He gave the show away with two words so familiar. "Why not?"

The woman's voice—"I keep telling you, I ain't sure. I got kids, and—" her voice broke a little—"and Joe ain't that bad." She had the rough, aggressive accents of a countrywoman. She said, and she was nearly crying, "Goddam, why did I have to meet up with you? Why can't you leave me alone? If you'd go away and stay away I wouldn't think about you soon. Then I'd be all right."

Pretty Boy found it interesting. It kept his mind off what people were saying about himself, and after that coke drink he wanted only to listen to distracting, soothing sounds. And what these other people in the cafeteria were saying wasn't soothing.

The man's urgent voice again, petulant, wanting something like more because it was being withheld from him. "Joe's too old for you. He don't treat you right. Me, I want to take you away, want to give you a good time. And you go and sit and look fit to bust out cryin'!"

Pretty Boy finished the second coke, got a third and a packet of food. It tasted good. He ate quickly, hungrily. Not stopping until the packet was empty. Then he got another out, and started in on that.

Some rough-voiced men came in just then. They got themselves cokes out of the machine and stood and drank them. All the time they talked about Pretty Boy. Pretty Boy, eating quickly in his corner, didn't dare turn, but he guessed they were newly-volunteered Vigilantes, by the way they talked.

And one let fall that the house-to-house search had already begun.

Pretty Boy ate on, but his mind was working rapidly, trying to think of some way out—and failing. The noose was tightening around him; there seemed no way of escape.

The men went quickly out again. Back of him the couple started in to talk. The man was grumbling, "You gotta make your mind up. I ain't coming all this way to Freshwater to see you no more. I gotta good house. a good job. I'll take you. It'll be easier for you than living way out where you never see a soul but your kids and Joe, day in and day out."

And still she couldn't make the decision. So he said, angrily, "What the hell, Thelma. You'd think it was this guy Pretty Boy who was tryin' to get you to go away with him!"

Pretty Boy sat and listened. The woman's reply was at a tangent. Perhaps she wanted a little more time before she made up her mind.

She said, "Him? A poor girl did go with him, didn't she?"

"A tart!" Contemptuously.

"A poor girl.... He must have been mad to have done what he did to her."

Pretty Boy suddenly found himself gripping the coke bottle, wanting them to go on—wanting to hear them say what his mind was beginning to tell him.

The man—"If he's mad, he don't need to worry much."

"He must be mad. You see, they'll find he's not sane to have done what he did. And they don't fry madmen...."

That was the idea that was beginning to flower in Pretty Boy's desperate brain. *They don't fry madmen!*

Then the woman was saying something, something

totally unexpected. "We'll know soon if he's mad. If they find another girl killed the same way, there won't be any doubt of it...."

The shock as the full import of what he was thinking hit him started to turn him round on his stool. Turned, so that he looked full into the woman's face. His mouth opened but said nothing. and then he pulled himself together and went out on to the crowded sidewalk.

After he had gone the man started to say. "What's Pretty Boy got to do with you and me and Joe?"

But she was staring out after Pretty Boy. Her face was incredulous, haggard—horrified. "Him," she whispered. "Didn't you see him?"

He was startled. The woman was nearly crying, for some reason. Then she pulled the newspaper out of his pocket and looked at the picture on the front; and the way she did it, it seemed that she didn't want to recognise the picture as being that of the cafeteria customer who had just gone quickly out.

She began to make a noise in her throat, and it wasn't pleasant to hear. The man saw that people were turning to look at him, and he got panicky, because this was a furtive visit to a Freshwater and you don't want attention at such times.

He said, "For God's sake, Thelma, what'n hell's bitten you?"

But she had slid off her stool and was crying—really crying. And she was beginning to shout hysterically, "That was him sittin' there just now—him...Pretty Boy! Pretty Boy was drinking cokes, then he just went out!"

They were all crowding round now, deserting their cokes and trays of cold food; they were talking, trying to talk above each other, and the waves of sound filled the small, bright cafeteria, and it sounded like a fight going on to people out on the sidewalk. They came crowding to the entrance, and then the word came out and travelled like wildfire down the street. "Pretty Boy's been seen. He was here less than a minute ago."

People were turning, trying to find Pretty Boy all along that brilliantly lit street. But now there were too many people rushing up, not knowing what the commotion was; it was easy for Pretty Boy to slide away without being detected.

And the woman inside the cafeteria was frantic now. The man with her tried to say, "Fer Crissakes, Thelma, d'you want Joe to know you've been up in town? Shut up, can't you—"

But the woman was sobbing, "I don't care about Joe. That doesn't matter. I saw Pretty Boy's face. He'd been listening to what we were saying. I gave him an idea.... God, I put the idea into his head! *I* did it!"

She was struggling now to get outside, to find a policeman. The man watched her with scared eyes, and then pushed out of sight into the crowd and out of her life.

She was screaming, and the crowd was taking up her words. She was crying, "Pretty Boy's going to kill another girl tonight! I saw it on his face. He's going to do it just the same way, so that we'll all think he's mad and they won't be able to fry him. He's going to tear another girl to pieces...."

A cop came just then. Around now there seemed to be plenty of cops in the street.

And a couple of blocks away a man had remembered a lightly made appointment with a girl by a clock tower at nine. It was two minutes to the hour, and recklessly, almost without heed to safety, he was plunging along the crowded sidewalks in an effort to be there on time.

CHAPTER TWELVE
ROADBLOCK CARNAGE

Lanny got a call through unexpectedly while he was up at HQ watching the streams of men drive up in cars to volunteer for the Vigilance Committee. He had hoped to get a few hundred; instead, they came by thousands. Every man was accepted. When they were identified they were sent out in parties under a cop. forming a circle that gripped tighter as it grew smaller in its steady approach to town. Every house, every shop, hotel, garage—every place was being searched and a Vigilante posted to see that no one unauthorised went back into the building.

Lanny was thinking: It can't be long now. With all these Vigilantes, we should be through Freshwater before midnight. Pretty Boy might just as well hand in his checks right now. Then he was called to the phone.

A familiar voice gravelled out. Lanny hadn't expected it. It was Boss Myrtle.

Boss said, "Bonnie?"

Lanny said, "Not a clue yet," and heard Boss sigh.

Then Boss began to say things, slowly, and Lanny couldn't believe what he heard at first.

"I'm quitting, captain." Boss Myrtle quitting without a fight! "You heard me tell my men to pack? Well, I meant it. I'm on my way out of Freshwater right now."

Lanny said, softly, "What's the idea? Until a few minutes ago you were the big cheese in Freshwater? What's turned you cold so suddenly, Boss?"

A pause, then a growl. "The hell, I don't like F.B.I. men. The chief told me what the Feds said to him about a town that had a racketeer running the police chief. When the Feds know so much, they've already begun to act. My guess is I'm going out one jump ahead of them. Me, I got no illusions about Feds."

Lanny said, still softly, "Who're you kidding, Boss? You gave that order to quit Freshwater before you'd spoken to the chief."

Boss's sigh came over the phone. "Okay, go right on thinking I'm kidding. But I'm goin' out—now!"

Lanny said, "It wouldn't be that you're going out to give Bonnie a chance, would it? You know she's bound soon to find you out for what you are, and it'll break her heart...."

Boss interrupted. "There's something in that, too, captain. In the last few hours I've realised a few things. One is that daughters grow up and want to live their own lives. Well, I love .my daughter." It took something to get those words out. "And I c'n see that she'll never have chance to get a decent man for a husband with Boss Myrtle around the joint. I'm goin'—because I ain't gonna see my daughter with a crook for a husband."

"It's no dice, being a big shot?"

"It's no dice when you see F.B.I. men starting in on you. When G-men get to trailin' you, you can already hear the clanging gates in that big concrete pen up river. I guess it's time to pull up my hooks and slide quietly away. I've had my life, I guess, and now it seems I'm only standing in the way of my daughter's happiness."

Lanny stirred uneasily. He disliked sentiment, and here he was getting an earful. He growled back, "I'm warning you, Boss. Just as soon as you're out of the way, I'm going to grab Bonnie and marry her. She's the girl for me. What do you know about that—and you hating the guts of me?"

Boss didn't answer for a while. Then he said, "I don't know, captain. No father likes to think of his daughter going to another man. But...well, I only hate your guts because you're a copper. Maybe Bonnie couldn't have a straighter man."

Lanny found himself saying, "Thanks, Boss," taken aback. And then Boss was saying he'd have to go. He wasn't going far for a while, not until he was sure of Bonnie's safety. But he guessed he couldn't do anything, just hanging around, and those F.B.I. men were already in town....

"Tell Bonnie everything, won't you, captain? Tell her if I can keep free, I'll come back and watch her sometime—maybe when you're not around I'll sneak up an' talk to her." There was a funny note in Boss Myrtle's gravel-wadded growl.

Lanny said, "There's just one thing, Boss. I guess

Bonnie's got her own account. Where does she bank?"

Boss was surprised. "Some place out at Green Hollow, I guess. The East Coast Bank, it'll be. Why? You thinking of marrying her for her dough?"

Lanny said, "No. It's something else. Maybe you'll know later." And there was apprehension in his voice. This small idea had been back of his mind for the last half-hour or so. Bonnie—it could be that that was the explanation of her mysterious disappearance. Maybe there was a girl inside that safe—Bonnie Myrtle! He went down and got in his car and drove furiously across to where the Navy men were still working....

If Boss Myrtle had known what was in Lanny's mind, he would have risked all the F.B.I. men and stayed on in Freshwater. As it was, he got behind the wheel and drove steadily out with his apes along the west road. He was going into hiding, but there was no need for panic....

* * * * * * *

Maxie Christman was up next to Dimenza as they drove westwards. For the first three miles they'd keep to the main road, then they would turn left down a track and bump their way by one dirt road after another out to the distant Coast Bypass. They would be beyond roadblocks then, and the way would be clear into New York—and safely!

When they thought of New York they grew nostalgic. They weren't used to small towns like Freshwater: without mighty skyscrapers and miles of streets they felt somehow exposed—naked.

They weren't far from where they had to turn off the main highway, when suddenly Maxie Christman swore and swung round in his seat. Marty Dimenza was already stamping on his brake.

"Trouble," grated Maxie, going for his gun. "A road block. Blast it, it's a trap," he shouted.

Someone ahead was swinging a lamp as a signal for them to slow down. The roadblock consisted of two long sedans, staggered parallel diagonally across the road. To get by you had to turn in between them, then pull round and straighten out. If you could do that at more than five miles an hour you were very good. Dimenza knew he wasn't that good. Anyway he was in a panic.

Marty was getting excited beside him, shoving a gun into his ribs and shouting again, "Blast it, you've taken us into a trap. You got ten grand for fixing things for us. What the hell sort of a fix is this?"

Eddy Eitel kept his head. He shouted, "Go back in reverse and turn, Dim. For Crissakes do something!"

Dimenza was slow, but he stopped the car so suddenly the nose nearly ploughed up the concrete highway; then he started back in reverse.

A cop came running out, gun in hand, shouting. Behind him were several Vigilantes with shotguns. Lanny had cunningly moved a few road blocks close up to the town, so as to cover the back roads with the few armed men he'd got. And the bank busters had driven blindly into the trap.

Eddy opened up from the rear seat, firing through the windscreen. Christman and Dimenza ducked as glass shattered all around them. The cop stopped running forward, and instead went back into the darkness much more rapidly. The Vigilantes, mostly old hoys, suddenly revealed unexpected powers as sprinters.

They were starting into speed, backwards, when something nearly as big as an elephant gun opened up from behind a hedge and a front tyre blew to ribbons. The car swung crazily and went off the road. Right then headlights fell on them as a big sedan came pulling up behind.

Eddy opened the door and tumbled out, snarling, "Run for it. We went into a trap!"

He fired at the headlights that were full on them, and glass shattered. Then a fusillade of revolver fire answered him back.

Something hit him in the shoulder and he lost his gun in the darkness as he ran out of the beaming headlights. He heard the others pounding off the road after him.

Then the Vigilantes opened up with their shotguns, and it sounded like a war had started. It wasn't too dark to see, just beyond the streaming lights, and Eddy ran towards a dim mass that could have been the shrubbery of a private park.

Maxie Christman, swearing savagely, was emptying his gun towards the sedan. Red fire prickled back, and lead screamed high and hateful all around him. He ran on, away from Eddy. Boy Fehse was also running away. Alan Ladd had suddenly gone off in a spiral of panic, leaving the others to fight it out.

Gino Lucci, fat and sagging, wasn't sure which way he was going. He fired a couple of times at the car, then turned to let off at the crouching Vigilantes. They beat him to it. Two or three shotguns let rip at the same moment. Probably all got him in the face with buck-shot. It was a good job he was thirty or forty yards away.

As it was, he clutched his face and started screaming. Then he started to stagger around sightlessly, never stopping his screaming, while the headlights of the big sedan behind streamed whitely on him. No one took any notice of him. No one took time off to try and get him under cover. Anyway, he was bawling so strongly everyone knew that he'd have strength to serve his time in the pen.

In the end he stumbled against the sedan, now empty save for the man behind the wheel. His hand came out and touched a rough coat. Gino moaned a mouthful of Italian and then whimpered. "For God's sake, why don't you do somep'n? They shot my eyes out, can't you see?"

But the driver didn't answer. He was dead. That first bullet of Eddy Eitel's had got him in the head.

And in a ditch a man with a military moustache and bearing was dragging a shattered leg and whispering, "Jesus Christ, we ran right into it. They got here quick, the Feds!"

* * * * * * *

Eddy rested against a fence. Someone was crawling along a ditch just below him, someone else was blundering through the bushes. Eddy had lost blood and couldn't move any more until he had rested. Back on the road there was still a bit of firing between the old boys with the sporting guns, and a couple of apes from the sedan. That was something that Eddy couldn't understand, but he didn't take time off to think about it.

He was watching the fellow crawling along the ditch towards him. The moon helped by coming out just then, and Eddy saw the bald head and sharp eyes of Marty Dimenza. With those long, flat cheeks he looked more like a rat than ever.

Bright came lolloping out of the bushes just then. He was grinning his inane, tooth-bared smile, and his eyes were going everywhere at once with excitement. He stopped, seeing Eddy against the fence, but didn't say anything.

Marty Dimenza must have heard the noise above him, but he was in a panic and kept right along that ditch. When he was directly under Eddy, the mob leader stepped down on to his neck.

It hurt and Dimenza started to struggle but Eddy said, "You keep still unless you want a hole in your head." It still went on hurting, with that boot back of his car, pressing his face into the soft wet earth, but Marty stopped struggling all at once.

Eddy hadn't a gun. but Bright was clinging to his. Eddy could see the shine from the moon on it, and he beckoned quickly for Bright to come over.

To Dimenza he was growling, "You were gonna fix it, huh? You took ten grand and you drove us right into a trap, yeah? You're a right nice sort of rat, Dim, and there's things that should be done to rats."

He was motioning to Bright, but Bright didn't catch on at first.

Dimenza panicked and his muffled voice came up, "Fer God's sake don't do nothing silly, Eddy! You know me! I wouldn't do a thing like that. Honest to God, I thought the roads were clear."

Eddy said, brutally, "Sure, you thought they were clear," The hell, why didn't Bright get what he was after! "You just drove straight up to a road block, and there was a carful of G-men on our tails all the way from town. How did they get on to us if they hadn't been tipped off? And who could have tipped 'em off? Only you, Dim, only you."

Bright was catching on. He came shambling forward and clambered into the ditch beside Eddy. His face was even more vacuous than usual under the white light of the moon. Eddy leaned back against the ditch wall, all his weight on the foot that kept Marty Dimenza face down. He hadn't strength to stand this much longer, but he wanted to hold up just another minute or so. He silently showed Bright what he wanted him to do.

Dimenza panicked, though he hadn't seen Bright. "I didn't do nothin', Eddy. I didn't tell no one."

Big, bony, empty-minded Bright was kneeling beside him now.

"You shouldn't think that of me, Eddy, not if you knew the trouble I took to fix things. I bin double-crossed...."

The muffled voice came up gaspingly. That foot was hurting. Dimenza had to move to rid himself of the pressure. Eddy, too weak to retain his balance, gestured frantically with his sound hand.

Bright put the gun to Dimenza's head, looked up with that soft grin of his, and pulled the trigger.

Eddy felt a spasm go through the body of Dimenza, and it jerked his foot off that fat neck and he slid down into the ditch. He would have stayed there, but Bright pulled him up and out and started to drag him into the trees beyond the fence.

Bright was saying. "That sure did for Dim, didn't it? Me, I like shootin' people. You got anyone else you want shootin', Eddy?"—eagerly. "Look, let's you'n me go and shoot a few more people, huh? Maybe a cop or two, yeah? Me, I got so I must shoot someone else. Goddammit, I gotta gun and I gotta kill somebody else, I tell yer!"

He let Eddy slip to the ground. He was shouting a lot, and they could hear him back on the road. Some of the Vigilantes came up running. Eddy lay there on the cool earth and felt the life spurting out of an artery. He was drowsy, tired. All he could think was: So what? I'll be dead in an hour, anyway. And it didn't seem so bad, death, just then to Eddy Eitel....

Bright started firing. Someone—probably the cop— opened up with a revolver, and then the old boys got going with sporting guns. It didn't take long. Bright stood there, grinning, until there was so much lead in his body that he couldn't carry the weight any more. And then his legs buckled, he fired for the last time, and that was the end of Bright, gunman and bank-buster.

CHAPTER THIRTEEN
SATIATION

Pretty Boy came down to the harbour road when his watch showed five after nine. Now he could see the tall clock tower rearing up along the crescent promenade, and it didn't look more than a couple of minutes' walk away. But it took him longer, much longer; appearances were deceptive. It was nearly a quarter after nine when he came up to Tissdan's big store opposite the clock tower.

He was almost running, the last few hundred yards, and it attracted attention, yet he no longer cared much. Probably he got away with it by his very boldness; because he was going so quickly that people hadn't time to see his face properly.

He saw her from across the well-lighted road. She was standing there waiting, and the way she looked around he could see she was annoyed because he wasn't there.

He started to cross the road, but a string of traffic was released by the lights and rushed him, and he had to skip back. When they had careered away, he ran quickly across the road, a smile of welcome and apology on his handsome face....

He saw her. She had given it up. She was swinging aboard a suburban bus, a disappointed, disillusioned girl who would weep into her pillow that night because such a handsome man had lightly led her up the garden path....

Pretty Boy's face contorted savagely, watching that bus career away. That girl who was to have died could have saved his life! That was how Pretty Boy thought of it; and he was furiously angry with the girl, and it seemed to him that she hadn't played fair by him.

He went walking off blindly down the broad side-walk. In his anger he didn't look where he was going at first, and then he bumped into a little man and nearly flattened him, and the fellow got angry and said things to him and attracted attention for the moment, and after that Pretty Boy pulled himself together and walked more carefully.

He didn't know where he was going, didn't care. All he knew was that he needed a girl if he were to save his life; and there weren't many walking the streets this night unaccompanied....

He came to a stop. He was outside a store that had a strong odour of antiseptics. He looked into it....

Alone in the shop was the white-smocked girl who had attended to his scratched neck that afternoon.

He went in. It was well-lighted and he knew he was taking a risk. But he felt pretty confident; shop assistants haven't time to look at pictures and follow the latest news like other citizens. And she wouldn't expect Pretty Boy to walk in so openly on her.

She looked at him, a smile of recognition on her face. Perhaps behind that smile was a faintly puzzled look also, the kind of look that comes when you feel you should recognise the person before you....

But she continued to smile, and that was good enough. Pretty Boy became at once pleasantly at ease.

"I thought I'd get a clean plaster on for the night," he smiled. "Would you oblige?"

She fluttered her eyelashes. When Pretty Boy smiled at a girl, it did things to her. She removed the plaster with those cool fingers.... Pretty Boy thought dispassionately that they might be a lot colder in an hour or two. Then another dressing was pressed gently into place.

When it was over and paid for, Pretty Boy lingered as though he found the company pleasant. And the girl lingered as though she found Pretty Boy's company attractive, too.

So Pretty Boy said softly, "It won't be long before you finish, I guess. How about you'n me eating out somewhere at one of the hotels."

The girl said, demurely, "I should love it—"

Pretty Boy's heart leapt. "Okay. Just say when I should come back for you."

But the girl was looking towards a glass partition. She said, again with that demure smile, "You'd better ask my—my husband that!"

Pretty Boy could have struck her down. She stepped back, shocked at the change that came over that handsome face. Abruptly he whirled and went out, leaving a shaken, startled white-faced girl to decide whether or not to tell her husband....

Out on the sidewalk, not so bright now that the shop lights were going out, Pretty Boy paused as he heard that familiar loud speaker.

"Here is a police warning. Attention, everybody, Pretty Boy has been seen again in Freshwater. Women are warned not to take up with strangers. This man is dangerous, and it is believed that he plans to kill another girl tonight. Women are warned...."

Pretty Boy stared after it aghast. It all seemed totally unfair to him; he felt aggrieved—they were making things difficult for him by putting women on their guard. What chance had he now of establishing this alibi of insanity? Rage mounted in him; he was snarling as he shoved off down the sidewalk. And then he heard another message from the loudspeaker.

"Attention all motorists! You are asked to put your cars on the streets with headlights on. We want you to light up every dark place in Freshwater. Pretty Boy needs a victim—and he also needs darkness. *Don't let him have either!*"

At once a brilliant light blazed into his face as a cooperative citizen down the road switched on the headlights of his parked car. Pretty Boy immediately turned up a side way that was poorly lit because it was in the warehouse area. He hadn't gone fifty yards up the deserted alley when his body suddenly threw a long shadow before him. A car had moved to the end of the alley.

Some way along he turned off right...and walked into the bright beam of car headlights. He turned back; he preferred a light that didn't shine on to his face.

Where the warehouses ended was a broad, desolate waste patch. He was skirting it when he saw headlights weaving into the sky. Then they steadied and settled and cut bright diverging paths into the darkness over the waste lot. A quarter of a minute later another car moved into position. By the time Pretty Boy came out on the other side, there was a ring of cars around the area, and it was so light it would have been like performing on the stage, to have done anything there.

The cars hadn't got around to the streets beyond. He was moving out into the suburbs now, and there weren't many people about. At the door of most apartment blocks were little groups of people talking. Pretty Boy guessed that among them would be police or Vigilantes, but he strode by quite openly and no one thought to challenge him.

He came up a hill that was pleasantly shrub-bordered, and he was feeling very desperate now. When he looked back, Freshwater glowed in a white halo as light reflected from hundreds of car headlights. And every minute the brightness crept nearer, as though it were following him.

He knew this couldn't last. It couldn't be long now before those advancing lights drove him on to the cordon of police and pickets, and they wouldn't let him through without carefully looking into his face.

Time was against him. Desperation gripped him

like a fever and sent him hurrying crazily along....

And suddenly he knew that the trail was ended. Knew it as soon as he saw the light fall on that face.

He was coming round a corner. A girl was crossing towards him; their paths were going to converge. She was a trim, slick little girl, as glamorous as a movie queen in her peroxide and lipstick and nylons.

And when he saw that face he knew her.

It was the girl who had served him at the cigar stand in the station that afternoon.

There were people about. Not many, but the street wasn't deserted, and that must have been reassuring. Maybe the girl would have cut and run if she'd found herself alone, addressed by a strange man on the night that Pretty Boy was known to be in town.

As it was, Pretty Boy struck the right note from the start. He was good at that.

He called cheerfully across to her, long before they came together. "Hyar, there! Sold all your Luckies?"

That was a good move. It seemed to suggest to the girl that here was a man who knew her, and you don't get scared of men who seem to know you well.

She seemed to relax. She wouldn't be able to see his face completely, but she'd see enough to please her. Pretty Boy had a pretty profile.

She showed him good teeth in a Hollywood smile. She was wearing plenty of lipstick. He didn't come close up to her as they went along the sidewalk, and a yard of space can be very reassuring to a girl out alone.

He was wondering if she had heard that police car;

wondering if she had come up out of town without hearing that warning to girls about strange pick-up men.

"You live around here?" he asked.

"Yeah," she said, smiling bigly. "Just up a coupla blocks." She was the kind that would chew gum if he offered some, he thought.

"Well," he said, wonderingly, "what do you know! I've been calling on you for Luckies this last week or two and wondering where you hide out, and now I find you right on my own doorstep." It was all very reassuring, he could see. And flattering. He said, "You remember me, don't you? The guy that always asks for Luckies?"

"Sure," she smiled, her face a gash of white teeth within over-red lips. "Sure, I always know you want Luckies when I see you come up."

Pretty Boy stopped worrying then. Didn't force the pace at all from that moment. Suddenly she stopped outside an apartment block. She pointed up to a lighted window and said, "That's where I live. That'll be mum, I guess. She'll be fixing things for supper, I guess." But she didn't go in.

Pretty Boy looked back at the brightening southern horizon. Those damned cars were lighting up the place all right; and they were coming nearer fast, as the news spread and citizens went to get their cars out. He looked across to where a street led down into the town opposite this apartment block. It was patchily lighted—yet.

He said, "They're after this Pretty Boy fellar. The

heat's on now. Bet they catch him any time! Me, I'd like to be around when they meet up with him." He dropped his voice to a savage growl. "I was goin' down to see what's cookin' in town when I met up with you."

She didn't rise to the bait. He started to turn away then hesitated. "You comin'?"

She hesitated, looking up at that lighted window.

"Don't you want to see Pretty Boy when they catch him?"

He could feel she was weakening. But she was still looking up at that light, as though it attracted her.

Pretty Boy said. "I'm off. I wouldn't miss this fun for anything!" He even stepped into the road, to complete the act, and now he was sweating. Those damn' car-headlights weren't far off now! It wouldn't be long before they shone on to him whichever way he looked.

She seemed to move a little towards him. "Aw, forget supper with mom!" He made it sound small-town stuff. "Look, come down with me and we'll cat out some place after we've seen Pretty Boy with the bracelets on. Yeah?"

The girl nodded, suddenly making up her mind. She went quickly forward after Pretty Boy. As they turned down the patchily lit street, a pair of blazing headlights turned into the road where they'd been standing. The hunt was rapidly closing in.

Light feet pattered along the sidewalk. Then they stopped. The light shone in that apartment window facing down the patchily lit street. A woman was putting cutlery out for the evening meal....

After a time someone went walking on...almost sauntering...along that patchily lit street.

And the fever was leaving Pretty Boy now. That wild, exultant thrill that had only once before in his life found climax, had found satisfaction yet again.

CHAPTER FOURTEEN
WHEN THE SAFE OPENED

Lanny stood in front of that massive safe door and spoke with the tired young Navy officer. He said, "There's a girl missing now. She banks here, at this branch. I've got a feeling—a bad one—that we'll find her inside."

The Navy man took his cigarette out of his mouth and turned, a question on his face. "A girl you know?"

"Yeah," Lanny nodded, looking at that mighty door, and then looking at the pathetic hole that had been burned into it after all these frantic hours. "Yeah," he said tiredly. "My best girl."

The officer looked hard at his cigarette and tried to think of something consoling. "I've seen cases before," he said. "A wrecked submarine down at Dagarra Reef. You'd be surprised how long they lasted in an atmosphere that seemed more sulphur-dioxide than oxygen. It's still a good chance they're alive in there right now."

Lanny said, "Maybe. Maybe you're right at that. But what are they gonna be like by the time you've got even an air tube through that door?"

The Navy man was silent. He couldn't think of

anything else to say, so he went across and took one of the burners, lit his cigarette from it and started to burn metal himself.

Lanny stuck around until he couldn't stand it any longer; then he went back to HQ so as to be there when things happened.

He was there when a message came that two cars had stopped at a roadblock and there was a gun battle going on. He was on his way in a radio car when they got a message through that it was all over....

He went to the roadblock, looked at the bodies lined up on the concrete, stood for a while and then went back into town. The cop who was at the roadblock said he thought that a couple of the hoods had got away— they could account the others. Lanny said he didn't think they'd last long, and he was looking at a town that threw a white aurora into the clear night sky. He was back at HQ, waiting for the next message, when a car came in bearing a wounded Maxie Christman, and a white-faced, suddenly terrified, Alan Ladd. Boy Fehse was wakening from a dream that had turned into a nightmare.

Then came a message that turned the building upside down; there was such an uproar, following it, it made previous commotions seem like whispering contests.

Everyone went running from room to room, shouting the message, telling each other. Then they got together and talked savagely, and then went rushing around again aimlessly, wanting to do something, yet not knowing what to do.

A radio call had come in from a patrol car.

Pretty Boy had struck again.

A car, cooperating in the hunt, had turned down a side street. The driver had got out, found himself looking at a body just within a deep doorway. He'd gone at once for the police.

New messages came through, building up the picture. It was a girl's body. It was still warm, and she couldn't have been killed more than a few minutes.

For she had been killed, there was no doubt about that. She had died shockingly in an agony she couldn't express because of the gag that had silenced her.

When he got the details, Lanny said, "That's Pretty Boy, all right. That's how the other kid died, back in New York."

Sergeant Aubie Gillis was there, his black eyebrows and red face always all the time mooning around Lanny. He'd become friendly in the last few hours, ever since rumours had gone around about the chief being on the slide...it wasn't going to do him much good, Lanny thought.

Gillis said, "That guy must be nuts. Only a screwball would do a thing like that. The hell, the worse these fellars are the more likely they are to save their necks."

Lanny said, "Maybe that's how he figured it. Maybe that's why this poor girl had to die. To give Pretty Boy a let-out. Maybe he was in Europe a few years back when another guy tried to do the same thing."

"What happened? Did he fry?"

Lanny said, with grim humour, "He didn't fry. *They*

stretched his neck a yard long! That's how they do things over there. But Pretty Boy—he won't get away with this screwball alibi. You bet your life they'll fix for him to fry!"

He went down the stairs. He was on his way to where they had found the girl. The description, as it came through, could have applied to any girl almost—any blonde, that is. And Bonnie was a blonde....

As he came to the desk, someone came shoving his way up through the crowd of people who were packing the parkway outside. He didn't wear a jacket, and he looked a fine, clean young man. He was smiling a quiet, pleasant, good-humoured smile as he spoke across the desk to the sergeant.

He said, "I'm Pretty Boy."

The sergeant said. "Sure, sure," and went on writing.

Lanny heard him and wheeled, looked into that face. He pulled his gun, but he didn't point it at Pretty Boy; it was directed at the door through which he could see that big, sullen mob milling.

He rapped, "You, sergeant, get down from that desk. Get this man safely into a cell, for Crissakes. The hell, if that mob know he's standing here we'll have a corpse on our hands—if we can fit the bits together!"

The sergeant took one look over his glasses, got it, and came heaving round. It was done so quickly that though they were in full view of hundreds of people, no one tumbled to it.

They got Pretty Boy into a cell. And Pretty Boy, listening to the roar that went up when the news got around outside, relaxed and thought how smart he had been. Those dumb clucks could roar their heads off; they couldn't get at him here.

They couldn't. But Uncle Sam could. And did....

* * * * * * *

Lanny called in the Vigilantes and sent his tired men home. He himself went to see the last victim of Pretty Boy and then drove on to Green Hollow.

It was a relief to find that the torn little corpse wasn't Bonnie, but it didn't dissipate the dread that was in heart as he came up to the bank—that Bonnie might be dying nearly as painfully right now....

He sat for half an hour and never took his eyes off the workers burning into the door. In time, because of the bright lights from the movie operators who had descended on the place, he got to imagining that the door was beginning to open. Only, every time he got up to say something he saw that the door was shut.

The Navy man next to him noticed it and said, "That's how it does things to me. Well, my guess is we've six more hours to wait yet before we even get a tube into them. It'll only be a few hours after that that it'll open itself."

Lanny said, "Yeah, that's how it looks to me. It doesn't make me feel good."

Scheer had joined them; his job was pretty well tied up by now. He said, sympathetically, "Your girl mightn't be in there, captain."

Lanny said, "So? Then where in heck is she?"

After that they sat for ten minutes, in silence. The door started doing tricks again.

After a time it got to doing tricks worse than ever before.

None of them said anything, because it seemed to be happening to all of them at the same time. The door seemed to be slowly opening. They'd seen that happen before. But this time it seemed to be opening wider than ever. Which was silly, because it wasn't timed to open before eight next morning, nearly ten hours from now.

And it even seemed to be swinging so irresistibly that it pushed the Navy burners back out of the way.

Scheer said, "My God, has something happened?"

Because they were looking inside the safe now, and back of them the cameras were clicking like mad and the radio commentators were screaming each other down to get their description of the scene out to the wide world of the American continent.

For they *could* see into the safe, and they saw a pile of bodies with one droop-shouldered man sitting stop them. Lanny saw it was Czanik, the Czech branch manager.

And saw he was alive.

Everyone went across in a rush and started to pull people out. Lanny was there, searching under the pile. When he straightened, for all the grisly sight there was relief in his heart. They were men, all of them, inside that safe. At least Bonnie Myrtle hadn't been shut up inside to die.

The waiting ambulance men came forward. There were eleven men inside. Two were dead, two others weren't far off. Miraculously, as the fresh night air poured in on them, the rest of the men moaned and stirred. As the Navy officer said, it was surprising what the human frame could stand.

Czanik even did a bit of talking. A kindly stretcher bearer eased him on to a blanket and said, "Lady Luck sure smiled on you tonight, openin' that door ahead of time."

Czanik stirred and said, "Lady Luck nothing. I saw what was coming. I shoved the janitor in front to cover me and I started turning back those dials. He had the sense to keep still, but they shoved us back before I got round to stops."

"A resourceful guy, like I said," Lanny commented, walking out with Scheer.

On the sidewalk, watching the ambulances fill, they hesitated. Scheer said, "That's finished me for the night. And you?"

Lanny was thinking of Bonnie. He said, "I'll go home for a shower, put on a clean shirt, then get back to duty. I'm not going to sleep until I know what's happened to Bonnie Myrtle."

As before, relief hadn't lasted long. Now gnawing doubts were in his mind. He was thinking that Pretty Boy could be mad. Could have killed someone else before the heat got too great. She could be lying around somewhere out of sight.

He moved quickly, to snap out of what he was

thinking, got into his car, and accelerated round to where his apartment was. He left the car out front and got into the self-operated elevator. Got to his apartment.

Bonnie was sitting there, dressed ready to go. Lanny heard her talking a long way off and sank down into a chair and didn't listen, but just looked at her and let gladness pick him up in her arms and hold him in a long-enduring kiss for moments on end.

It didn't matter that Bonnie was alternating between sulks and bad temper, saying things to hurt him. The one important thing was that Bonnie, for whom the town had been turned upside down, was here, alive and well, in his apartment...from the sound of it had been here all this time!

He stopped her as she was putting on the old act of flouncing out of the door. If she'd meant it, she'd have done it long ago, of course; she'd had plenty of time.

He said, "Tell me, how did you get in here?"

"How?" There was disdain on that pretty, pink and cream face. "I asked the janitor to let me in. When he looked doubtful, I just smiled at him."

"Sure, sure, I get it." Somewhere back of his mind he was remembering someone had said something about being wanted out at home. Murdoch, of course, down by the pier head. But he hadn't grasped it at the time. It had got confused with the chief's telling him to pack up and go home....

He said, "There's no fool like an old fool," and he was thinking of the susceptible, middle-aged janitor.

Bonnie found herself being pulled back into the room. "You've never been here before, Bonnie. Why did you come?" He was wondering how to break the news to her.

She got a handkerchief out and that meant she was contemplating tears. Lanny thought there'd be plenty tears soon enough and didn't try to talk her out of it. She stamped her foot, which was the right thing to do in her mood and said, "I hate you, oh, I hate you!" which was also right for the occasion.

"Sure," said Lanny, putting his arm round her. "I know you do. Sitting here all afternoon and evening, sure I'd come home any time, and me not turning up until now. It's sure hard on the morale, isn't it?"

She melted, right on his chest. Sobbed, "Oh, Lanny, you big brute, I waited and waited. The longer I waited the more I determined to stay here until—until I starved if need be! I—I don't know what daddy will say when I get back. Perhaps he hasn't missed me."

Lanny kept quiet on that subject. He was framing his first sentence....

She wept, "Lanny, darling, you don't know how I've suffered this last week. You won't see me now, won't even speak to me. I had to come. Lanny. Please, why must you always run out on me? Am I repulsive to you?"

Lanny sighed. "You've always known you're not. You're my best girl.... Honey, you don't have to go home tonight. You can stay here and I'll get another room."

Her head came up. There was something wrong and she knew it. "What is it, Lanny? You don't want me to go home."

Lanny sighed and said, "It just means someday when you're ready, you can become Mrs. Lanny Just." And then, as gently as he could, he told her a few things.

Very gently, that a man found shot behind the wheel of a big sedan was Boss Myrtle....

ABOUT THE AUTHOR

GORDON LANDSBOROUGH was born in 1913 in Huddersfield, Yorkshire, England. On leaving school at fourteen to help support his family, he attended night classes, eventually becoming a chemist with the research department of ICI. Continuing his studies, he turned to journalism and worked on a number of papers and journals in the north of England. In 1938, he started up *ARP News*, a magazine promoting air raid precautions to a war-nervous England.

He moved to London in 1939, and in 1940 he started up *Reveille* as the official newspaper of the Ex-Services' Allied Association. It was bought by the Mirror Group in 1947.

In 1940 he joined up with the London Scottish Regiment, serving for a time in the deserts of North Africa. Many years later his experiences would be incorporated into a number of bestselling war novels.

Returning to London, in 1949 he was appointed editor of Hamilton & Co. (Stafford) Ltd, a very undistinguished lowly publisher of pulp fiction. With Landsborough at the helm, the publisher soon took a turn for the better. In 1951 he rebranded them as

'Panther Books', publishing a regular series of all types of genre novels, most notably science fiction, and he also launched the famous British SF magazine, *Authentic Science Fiction*. As part of his editorial duties, Landsborough wrote numerous westerns, crime, and foreign legion thrillers, mostly under his personal pseudonym of Mike M'Cracken. His own personal memoirs on this period of his career can be found in the book *Vultures of the Void: The Legacy* by Philip Harbottle.

In 1954 Panther Books became one of the leading British publishers, switching from original genre novels to paperback reprints of bestselling hardcover novels from other publishers. Their format was improved, and only the finest cover artists were hired, including in particular "Cy Webb" (Reginald Heade) and "Peff" (Sam Peffer), Harold Johns, and Josh Kirby. Nonfiction titles predominated, especially Second World War books, and the fiction titles were by famous bestselling writers, internationally known.

Landsborough had earlier tsken a break from Hamiltons to pursue his own career as a writer, eventually producing about 100 books over the next thirty-five years. His publishing expertise was well known within the trade, however, and he was employed as an advisor to several publishing companies

In 1957 Landsborough started up Four Square Books, backed by Godfrey Phillips, the tobacco company. Michael Geare, who was employed by him in 1957 as sales manager, said of him that "He was a gifted, clever, likeable chap, and really knew everything about book publishing. On one occasion when we were a book short on the list, he took five days off and wrote the book himself. It wasn't half a bad paperback, either." Four Square Books was very successful, and were sold to New English Library in 1962.

Landsborough went on to create several successful imprints, most notably the children's paperback company, Armada Books (later bought out by Collins Books), The Armada Books list included, somewhat controversially, Enid Blyton, whose books at that time was frowned on by libraries and academics, but still sold in their hundreds of thousands. His list also included his own adaptations for children of the *Tarzan* and the *Beau Geste* series of books, and stories written for children based on the popular television series *Bonanza*.

Later in the 1960s he started up another children's publishing company, Dragon Books. This was also acquired by Collins (Armada).

Always a very generous and public-spirited man, during the 1960s Gordon Landsborough helped several charities and friends set up publishing ventures, including Trust Books, New Zealand Books, and Viking Books.

During this time he continued writing, including a dozen books under his own name, the bes-selling of which in 1956 was *Tobruk Commando*. In 1956 he also published a book about the *Battle of the River Plate* with sales revenue going to the survivors' fund, and in 1961 (under the pseudonym Alan Holmes) the book of Tony Hancock's film *The Rebel*. In the 1970s he continued to write, producing another five books, including the popular *Glasshouse Gang* series.

In the early 1970s he worked on freelance publishing ventures in Hong Kong and Australia involving tourism and travel.

In the mid 1970s he returned to England and turned his hand to bookselling, opening up a remainder book-selling business, *Bargain Books*. This mushroomed into a highly successful business, with four stores.

Throughout his life, as well as helping friends and family set up publishing and bookselling businesses, Gordon Landsborough spent much of his spare time helping charitable causes, particularly for war veterans. In the late 1970s he bought a large shop in Staines and, at his own expense, turned it into a community centre for senior citizens.

He held strong views about many social and political issues and actively campaigned for many of them, such as the Campaign for Nuclear Disarmament.

Gordon Landsborough died in 1983, aged 70, survived by three sons and two daughters.

In recent years several English publishers have been reissuing the best of his western and crime and foreign legion novels, and many of his dynamic detective thrillers are being published in the USA for the first time by The Borgo Press.